KLAW #2:

TOWN
OF BLOOD

W. L. Fieldhouse

TOWER BOOKS   **NEW YORK CITY**

Dedicated to Mrs. Margaret L. Fieldhouse, my dear mother, with love.

A TOWER BOOK

Published by

Tower Publications, Inc.
Two Park Avenue
New York, N.Y. 10016

Copyright © 1981 by Tower Publications, Inc.

<<<<<<<<<<<<<<<<<<<<<<<<<<<<<<<<<<<<<<<<<<<<<

"Drop your guns and cut him down!" Klaw demanded, raising his right arm. The converted Colt revolver was screwed into a brass base at the end of his arm by a threaded bolt; the bolt was attached to a copper ball that replaced the weapon's grips. Klaw's left hand hovered over the hammer.

"You're bluffing, Mister One-Hand," Pierce scoffed. "Ain't nobody can accurately fan a six-gun."

"You willing to bet your life on that, feller?" Klaw asked flatly.

"I thought you were moving on, Mister . . ." Clayton began.

"The name's Klaw. I thought you fellers were about to lynch a rapist. I guess we were both mistaken."

Suddenly the two men reached for their guns. Klaw's hand slapped the Colt's hammer rapidly, and there were two more dead men beneath the hanging tree.

Don't miss the first in this action-packed series by
W. L. Fieldhouse:

KLAW (Tower 51586)

Chapter One

xxooooooooooooooooooooooooooooooooooooooooooooooo

Klaw didn't generally get involved in other people's business. Riding across Texas, heading west because it was as good as any other direction, Klaw had enough problems of his own without picking up anyone else's. Still, some things a man can't ignore. A lynching is one of them.

In the middle of a grassy plain, five men were gathered around a large oak tree. Three wore dirty work shirts and levis, their appearance suggesting that they were ranch hands. A hemp rope with a hangman's noose dangled from a sturdy tree limb. While the trio placed the victim of the impromptu hanging on the back of a chestnut Morgan, the fourth man watched the proceedings with approval. He wore a lightweight cotton suit and clean white stetson. A tall man with broad shoulders and a wide chest, he sat astride a handsome Appaloosa, both hands resting on the saddle horn.

"Don't worry about putting the knot behind his ear, Pierce," he announced in a gruff voice. "Let him strangle slow."

"Sure thing, Mister Clayton," one of the cowboys replied as he mounted a sorrel. A lean, rawboned character with a rat-like face, Pierce smiled maliciously, revealing large yellow teeth.

The lynch victim was the most striking figure of the group. Coils of heavy muscle visibly strained against the fabric of his shirt and denim trousers. Although bruises and bleeding cuts marred his tan face, the man's Latin features were ruggedly handsome. A large humped spine flawed his otherwise perfect physique.

Pierce slipped the noose around the hunchback's neck. Giggling like a love-sick girl, he whispered, "You've had it, Lazaro! But don't worry, I'll take care of Sally after you're gone."

"*Senor* Clayton," Lazaro said, ignoring Pierce. "Do not do this thing. I am innocent . . ."

"Shut up, hunchback!" Pierce snarled as he drove a fist into Lazaro's kidney.

"I reckon even you, Lazaro, have a right to make your peace with God," Clayton remarked. "Maybe the All Mighty will take into consideration that you were born a cripple and show you some kind of mercy before tossing your soul into Hell."

Klaw urged his roan gelding forward. "Good morning," he called cheerfully.

They turned and stared at the newcomer. Klaw was over six feet tall, a lean man with a long, gaunt face. Although his skin was browned and leathered, his sunken cheeks indicated that he'd recently suffered a prolonged illness. He wore a dark denim shirt, levis and boots without spurs. Clayton and

6

his men were relieved to see the button flap holster on his left hip; the stranger was no gunfighter.

"Why spoil such a nice sunny day," Klaw said, smiling, "with a lynching?" He pushed back the brim of his tan stetson with the curve of a large steel hook attached to the end of his right arm.

The men stared at the metal extremity with surprise. Then Pierce shouted to the two cowboys on foot. "Luke, Matt!"

One of the hired hands reached for a rifle in the saddle boot, the other man dropping his hand to his holstered sidearm.

"Wait!" Clayton ordered sharply. "This is private property, mister," he told Klaw. "You're trespassing."

"Then I apologize," Klaw said, "but you don't have any fences or signs up. Before I ride on, however, I'd like to know why you fellers are stringing this jasper up. Is he a cattle rustler?"

"What business is it of yours?" Pierce demanded.

"Just like to know if I'm passing by justice or a crime. Sometimes, it's hard to tell them apart." Klaw calmly placed his hook in his left palm. With a sharp twist, he began to unscrew the steel extremity.

"This man—Lazaro Santos is his name—tried to rape my daughter," Clayton said through clenched teeth. "My foreman, Neil Pierce, saw it happen. Not that any of this is your damn business!"

"It is not true, *Senor*," the hunchback told Klaw. His sentence was a flat statement.

"You got a soft-spot for rapists, Mister One-Hand?" Pierce sneered, his fingers resting on the butt of his holstered .44 Colt revolver.

"No, I don't like rapists any better than I like loud-mouth bastards like you." Klaw answered mildly as he tucked his hook into his gunbelt.

"You lousy cripple! I ought'a blast you for that!" the foreman hissed, tightening his grip on the Colt.

"Pierce!" Clayton snapped. "If you want to kill a man for insulting you, you'll do it on somebody else's land!" Turning to Klaw, he added. "Now, if we've satisfied your curiosity, you'd best be moving on before Pierce decides to go ahead and put a bullet in you. Unless, of course, you reckon to protect this hump-backed son of a bitch."

Klaw shrugged. "If a man tried to force himself on a woman, I figure he deserves a rope dance, no matter who gives it to him."

Klaw prepared to move on when the sound of hoofs drew their attention. A blonde girl mounted on a piebald mustang galloped toward them. "Father!" she cried. "Stop, Father!"

Klaw slowly unbuttoned his flap holster.

"Sally! I told you to stay home!" Clayton growled. "This is no place for you, girl!"

An attractive young woman, her shapely figure admirably filling her riding clothes, exclaimed, "You mustn't do this! Lazaro is innocent! You can't hang him, please!"

"Do not beg for my life, Sally," the hunchback said quietly. "You have brought me all the joy I have ever known. If my life is to end now, I can die happily if I know you will be all right."

"Pretty speech for a humpy freak, ain't it?" Pierce chuckled.

Sally pulled on her reins, bringing her mustang to a halt. "Pierce lied to you, Father. He wants me for himself. You know he wants to inherit the

8

ranch, and this is how he plans to do it! I love Lazaro, Father . . ."

"Silence!" Clayton snapped angrily.

"No." Sally moved her mount closer to her father. "Lazaro wasn't doing anything to me that we hadn't done before. He's made love to me many times . . ."

The back of Sam Clayton's hand struck her violently across the face. Her head snapped back and she nearly fell from the saddle. The hunchback called out her name. Pierce punched him in the kidney again.

"Don't remind me what a harlot you've become, girl! Don't embarrass me by announcing your whoring in front of my men and this stranger." Clayton gestured toward Klaw as he spoke.

He stopped suddenly and stared into the muzzle of a .45 Colt.

"Drop your guns and cut him down!" Klaw demanded, raising his right arm. The converted Colt revolver was screwed into a brass base at the end of his arm by a threaded bolt; the bolt was attached to a copper ball that replaced the weapon's grips. Klaw's hand hovered over the hammer.

"You're bluffing, Mister One-Hand," Pierce scoffed. "Ain't no body can accurately fan a six-gun!"

"You willing to bet your life on that, feller?" Klaw asked flatly.

"I thought you were moving on, Mister . . . ?" Clayton began.

"The name's Klaw. I thought you fellers were about to lynch a rapist. I guess we were both mistaken."

9

"I told you what I seen this hunchback try to do to Miss Sally," Pierce insisted.

"I also heard that girl say Lazaro didn't attempt to rape her, so I figure she knows what happened better than you."

"Well, I reckon she feels sorry for the poor critter." Pierce shrugged.

Suddenly, the other two ranch hands acted. Matt Baldwin dragged his revolver from its leather, and Luke Jenner jerked his saddle gun from its boot. Klaw's hand slapped the Colt's hammer rapidly. A heavy forty-five bullet crashed into the center of Matt's chest, piercing his sternum and exploding his heart. The other cowboy had just jacked a round into his Winchester's chamber when Klaw's second .45 slug tore into the top of his forehead, burrowing into Luke's skull.

Pierce had cleared leather when Klaw's Colt stared into his startled face. The foreman dropped the pistol as if it was red hot and lifted his arms above his head.

"You still think nobody can hit anything by fanning a revolver, feller?" Klaw asked.

Pierce shook his head. Klaw watched Clayton out of the corner of his eye. The rancher sat in the saddle, his face a mixture of frustration and rage.

"If my arthritis hadn't crippled up my fingers so bad, I'd shoot you myself, Klaw!" he growled. "I still might!"

"But not right now," Klaw commented. "Cut him down, Pierce, or I'll cut *you* down."

The rodent-faced foreman nodded eagerly and drew a Bowie knife, cutting the rope above the noose knot and then sawing through the bonds at Lazaro's wrists. The hunchback rode from under

10

the tree towards Klaw.

"Don't get between either Pierce or his boss and me," Klaw warned. The hunchback followed his instructions.

"Apparently you don't know who I am, Klaw," the rancher said. "My name is Samuel Clayton and I own the largest spread in this county. I've got thirty seven men on my payroll." He stared down at the bullet-riddled corpses of Luke and Matt. "Thirty five, thanks to you. Most of my boys are pretty good with a gun. Not as good as you, maybe, but there's a lot of them and only one of you. Think about that before you ride off with that hunchbacked greaser. You're dealing yourself a lot of trouble."

"Won't be the first time, feller," Klaw replied simply. He watched the surviving members of the lynch gang carefully as Lazaro and Sally galloped up beside him. "Go on ahead," he told them. "I'll catch up with you in a minute."

The hunchback and the girl urged their mounts and took off. Pierce spat angrily. "You ain't seen the last of us!"

"Maybe." Klaw shrugged. "Just remember I handle a gun," raising the converted Colt at the end of his right arm, "as if it were part of my hand."

He tugged his reins to steer his horse toward the departing couple and broke into a gallop.

Chapter Two

Lazaro Santos removed the severed noose from his neck as he and Sally Clayton waited for their one-handed rescuer in some grazing land roughly a quarter of a mile away. Klaw galloped into view, his Colt still attached to the end of his arm.

"I don't know how to thank you, Mister Klaw," Sally said, dabbing a handkerchief at Lazaro's bloodied face.

"Just Klaw, ma'am," the tall man replied. "Everybody in one piece?"

"We are fine, *Senor*, but I fear you may regret your actions today," Lazaro told him. "Although I am very grateful to you for saving my life, I must warn you that Sam Clayton is not a good man to have for an enemy, and he is not the sort of man to forget what you did today."

"My father is a very proud man, Klaw," Sally explained. "He'll track you down and kill you if he can."

"What about you two?" Klaw inquired. "If you figure your daddy will be after my hide, then Lazaro is an even more likely candidate for retribution."

"*Si*," the hunchback nodded. "Sally is *Senor* Clayton's only daughter. He hates me for being her lover. Perhaps his anger is justified. Who would want their daughter to marry a *monstruosidad*? A freak with a crooked spine?"

"No, Lazaro," the girl insisted. "You are not a monstrosity or a freak."

"If you do not consider me one, that is all that matters." He smiled.

"Do you folks have any place to go?" Klaw asked. He placed the reins in his teeth as he opened the loading gate of his Colt and removed the two spent shell casings. Pocketing them, he replaced the revolver chambers with fresh cartridges.

"*Si*." Lazaro nodded. "I am the blacksmith in the town of Cercano Afeitar."

"Close Shave?" Klaw remarked with surprise.

"Ah, you speak Spanish, *Senor*?" the hunchback inquired.

"I was in Mexico recently," Klaw answered, painfully recalling his involvement with Elana Sojeda. "But I only learned a few words."

"A few are better than none," Lazaro assured him. "Yes, the town of Cercano Afeitar was founded by a barber from the great state of Boston. It was sort of a joke with him."

"How far is Cercano Afeitar from here?"

"Three miles, more or less. It is a nice, quiet town with peace-loving people."

"Sounds like the sort of place I could stand to spend some time," Klaw remarked thoughtfully, "providing it doesn't cost much to live there."

"Oh, no. Everything is very cheap. You don't have much money, *Senor*?"

"If a feller had to buy the air he breathes, I'd be dead by now."

"Well, you can stay in the livery stable if you wish."

"One of the best things to be said about a town can be summed up in two words, Lazaro—feather bed." Klaw smiled. "I got enough to buy a night or two in an inexpensive hotel. I might have to skimp a bit on meals, but my diet isn't anything fancy in the first place."

"I will be happy to have your company in Cercano Afeitar. I just hope we will not have any problems from Sally's father."

"Her father doesn't worry me, friend," Klaw stated. "But those thirty-five gunmen on his payroll might be a bit of a nuisance."

"*Si*," Lazaro nodded. "A nuisance that can make a fella very dead." He rubbed his throat where the rough hemp rope had chafed the skin.

"Yeah," Klaw muttered. "They're a real pain in the neck."

The trio rode into the town of Cercano Afeitar. The little community reminded Klaw of a dozen other small hamlets he'd encountered throughout the Southwest. Few of the buildings reached two stories tall. The bank and the jailhouse were made of brick. The other wooden structures had been designed in the simple and practical manner common to such towns. As they entered Cercano Afeitar, Klaw counted sixteen buildings—including private homes—in the entire town.

14

Lazaro led them to the livery stable. One of the largest establishments in Cercano Afeitar, it included both the blacksmith shop and the feed store. A small, painfully thin figure swept the plank walk in front of the feed store. Dressed in trousers, vest and shirt—all two sizes too large for his emaciated frame—the little man glanced fearfully at the one-handed stranger and his companions. Lazaro waved at him.

"*Buenos dias*, Albert," he greeted.

"Uh, hello, Lazaro," the storekeeper replied, nervously working his fingers along the shaft of the broom. "I'm glad you . . . you made it back."

"*Si*," the hunchback smiled pleasantly. "Thanks to this gentleman." He tilted his head towards Klaw. "He saved my life. He is a very brave *hombre*."

"That's . . . er . . . right nice, Lazaro." Albert nodded woodenly. His eyes widened with amazement as he watched Klaw unscrew the .45 revolver from the end of his arm. "Oh, lordy," he gasped.

"Never know what a feller has up his sleeve, huh?" Klaw remarked dryly, as he holstered the converted Colt and inserted the hook into the brass base.

"If you do not object, Albert," Lazaro said. "I'm going to give Klaw free use of the stables for his horse. If you insist, I will pay for this myself. After what he has done, it is the least I can do to express my gratitude."

"Oh, sure," Albert bobbed his head vigorously. "That'll be fine."

Klaw, Lazaro and Sally dismounted. Before they could lead their animals into the livery stable, a voice called to them.

"Wait a minute!" A rotund figure waddled

15

across the street to the trio. The fat man's face was decorated by a drooping gray mustache, bushy eyebrows and crowsfeet. His massive belly quivered over his gunbelt as he almost-ran to meet them. Sunlight flickered on the copper plated badge pinned to his vest.

"Howdy," he greeted, trying to catch his breath. "I'm not as young as I used to be."

"Nobody is," Klaw muttered.

"That's true enough," the lawman agreed with a weak smile. Looking at Lazaro, he said, "I'm glad to see you and Mister Clayton managed to come to an agreement. It's good to see you again, Miss Sally," he added, touching the brim of his sweat stained stetson.

"We didn't really reach an agreement, Sheriff," the hunchback replied. "Klaw convinced him to let me go."

"Klaw?" the fat man blinked. "Oh, this feller!" he turned to the one-handed man. "I'm Sheriff Cole Winn. Me and my deputies are paid to keep the peace in this town."

"Doesn't look like you've got a very tough job, feller," Klaw remarked.

"Not most of the time," Winn admitted. "We've got a nice quiet town here, with good, honest, God-fearing people. You won't hardly ever see a man walking our streets wearing a gun. That's the way we like to keep it."

"A gun is only as good or as bad as the feller using it, Sheriff," Klaw told him. "And this is one feller that plans to keep his." His hard gray eyes glared at Winn. "Is there a law against a man carrying a weapon in Cercano Afeitar? If there is, I think I'll camp outside of town."

"No, no," the lawman shook his head, loose

16

jowls trembling. "We just . . . well, don't encourage folks to pack an iron. There's too much violence in Texas as it is, and we figure the less guns around the better."

"That's crap!" Klaw snapped. "If I hadn't had a gun, Clayton and his men would have lynched Lazaro. If I hadn't been armed they would have shot me for interrupting their vigilante 'justice.' "

"You didn't shoot any of Mister Clayton's men, did you?" Winn inquired fearfully.

"Go ask him," Klaw growled. "While you're at it, ask yourself why you weren't out there trying to stop that lynching from happening. I figure the whole town knew about it, and you damn sure did. Where were you when they were putting a noose around Lazaro's neck?"

"That happened outside of town. Outta my jurisdiction," the lawman insisted.

"More crap," Klaw snarled. "You're the sheriff. That means you were elected to protect the citizens of this county. Don't tell me Clayton's ranch isn't part of your jurisdiction."

"Well, I don't appreciate you tellin' me how to do my job, young feller!" the sheriff huffed. "You just make sure you don't misbehave while you're in Cercano Afeitar, or you'll be seeing the inside of my jailhouse!"

Winn waddled away from them angrily. Lazaro looked up at Klaw and sighed. "You sure make enemies faster than friends," he observed.

"Everybody has a talent for something." Klaw shrugged.

After putting his horse away in the livery stable, Klaw wished Lazaro good luck and headed for the local hotel. A balding, middle-aged clerk nervously

17

greeted the tall stranger. He stared at the steel hook attached to Klaw's arm with consternation.

"I'd like a room, feller," he explained as he glanced around the hotel lobby which was bare except for the front desk. A narrow staircase led to the next floor.

"Oh? Just for the night?" the uneasy clerk asked, obviously hoping the one-handed man would confirm the question with an affirmative answer.

"How much will it cost?"

"For one night? Er . . . fifty cents."

"Then relax," Klaw said dryly. "You'll only have to put up with me for tonight."

"Of course . . . that is, all right, sir," the clerk stammered. "Room fifteen is available."

He handed Klaw a key. "If you'd like a hot bath I'll tell my sons to heat up some water for you."

"Sounds good, feller. Thanks."

"You go on up and get settled, sir," the clerk said, as he hurried out the door. "Bob and Jim will be up with the bath water in a jiffy."

Klaw sighed. So many people were unnerved by the sight of his artificial hand. He'd never realized how judgments were made solely on one's appearance until he'd lost his right hand nearly a year before. Perhaps that was one of the reasons he'd come to the aid of Lazaro Santos. The hunchback, like himself, was an oddity and a social outcast. A freak.

The sound of a hard object striking wood drew his attention to the stairway. Klaw looked up to see a figure limping down the steps. The man leaned heavily on the railing as he clomped down the stairs. He was an inch or two short of six feet tall, broad shouldered and muscular, with a powerful upper-torso. He wore dark levis, black riding boots, a red flannel undershirt, and—his most notable garment—a Confederate gray tunic with a lieutenant's bar on each shoulder. The wide brim of his stetson concealed most of his face as he awkwardly descended the stairs. Klaw wondered if the man might be drunk, but he noticed the right leg was held stiffly, its frozen foot striking each step hard. A .45 caliber Tranter revolver was on the man's right hip and a sheath knife on his left. Limping to the last step, the man raised his head. His wide face was nearly lost amid a dense beard and mustache. Fierce blue eyes glared at Klaw. The one-handed man shrugged. The ex-Confederate didn't interest him. The War Between the States had been over for ten years, and he had enough problems without tangling with a belligerent Johnny-Reb. Moving around the man, Klaw began to mount the stairs. Neither man uttered a word.

"Becker!" a voice shouted.

Klaw turned to see two men in the doorway. The pair wore ill-treated cattlemen's slickers, their clothes coated with a dusty film from the trail. One of them was barely five and a half feet tall, with a lantern jaw, large yellow teeth and a hawk nose, flanked by two hard black eyes. He held a .44 caliber Remington revolver in his fist. The other man was almost a foot taller than his partner. The floppy brim of his ten gallon hat covered most of his narrow face except the small, tight-lipped mouth and the abbreviated chin. An old Colt revolving rifle was in his bony hands. Both newcomers aimed their weapons at the man in the Confederate jacket.

"Tom Becker," the shorter figure snapped. "You drop your gun and come along with us, or me and Marty will drag you outta here with a couple slugs in yore carcass!"

"Right, Lonny," the taller gunman replied, revealing even worse tobacco stained teeth than his partner's.

"Don't you fellers have your states a little mixed up?" the ex-Reb commented, holding his right hand high and awkwardly dragging his Tranter from its leather with his left. "I'm not wanted in Texas."

Lonny smiled and revealed more ugly teeth. "We're gonna haul yore ass back to Arkansas, Becker. The wanted posters say dead or alive. It's all the same to us either way."

"Figured that," Becker remarked, his revolver falling to the floor.

Adroitly, his left hand plucked an Arkansas Toothpick from its belt sheath. Tossing the big Bowie to his right hand, Becker caught it by the double-edged blade. His arm swung rapidly, hurling the knife. Marty, the taller bounty hunter, screamed as the sharp point of the Arkansas Toothpick slammed into his chest. The blade sunk deeply through Marty's flesh, chipped his sternal bone and pierced the left ventricle of his heart. The bounty hunter pulled the trigger of his revolving rifle as he fell backward through the doorway. The .44-40 caliber lead-ball blasted a harmless hole in the ceiling.

Although Lonny was startled by Becker's sudden violent actions and alarmed by the gush of blood from his fatally wounded partner, his Remington roared. Becker, however, had already launched himself over the counter of the front desk, moving with remarkable speed for a man with a damaged leg. The bounty hunter's bullet sizzled an inch away from Becker's hurtling form, tugging at the coat tails of his Confederate tunic. The Johnny-Reb fell down behind the desk.

"You may as well come out, Becker!" Lonny snarled, his eyes narrowing as he cocked the Remington's hammer. "You left yore gun on the floor and yore knife in Marty. You're gonna pay for that, you bastard, but I'll go easy on you if you come out right now!"

Lonny carefully approached the side of the desk, his revolver held ready. Suddenly, Becker's arm swung around the top of the counter. A .32 caliber Smith & Wesson revolver in his fist fired twice. The startled bounty hunter staggered backward as the slugs tore into his chest. Blood staining his slicker, Lonny sunk to his knees, his Remington tumbling from numb fingers to the floor. Becker gripped the desk as he rose and limped forward, the smoking S&W in his hand.

"Help me!" the wounded bounty hunter pleaded, blood bubbling from his lips. "I can't breathe. God, it hurts! Please, help me."

"Sure enough," Becker muttered. He lowered the muzzle of his .32 and shot Lonny in the forehead.

Klaw watched the ex-Confederate raise his gray tunic and slip the diminutive S&W revolver into a holster at the small of his back. Kneeling by the dead bounty hunter, Becker quickly searched the corpse. He found a crumpled wanted poster and grunted with satisfaction.

"It's a lousy picture of me anyway," he remarked, as he stuffed it into the pocket of his jacket.

Becker suddenly realized that the one-handed

21

man had observed the entire melee from the stairwell. He glared up at Klaw and rasped, "You figure this is any of your business, feller?"

"Not really," Klaw replied mildly. "But it beat the hell out of any minstrel show I've seen lately."

The corners of Tom Becker's mouth turned up slightly, almost creating a smile. Sheriff Winn waddled to the entrance, a Dragoon pistol quivering in his unsteady grasp.

"Oh, God!" the fat lawman exclaimed, his lips and his face bleached pale by fear. Stepping over the corpse of Marty in the doorway, he entered the lobby. "Oh, no! Another one!" he said, gazing down at the dead bounty hunter on the floor.

"Glad to see you, Sheriff," Becker announced as he picked up his Tranter and returned it to the holster on his hip. "I'd like to report a shooting."

"You done this, Mister?" Winn asked Becker.

"That's right. Now put that gun away before you rattle the cylinder right out of the frame."

"Don't sass me, feller!" the sheriff said, trying to sound commanding, but his trembling voice ruined the effect. "I wanna know what happened here."

"These men drew on me." Becker shrugged.

"Why?" Winn inquired.

"Ask them." The ex-Confederate smiled without mirth.

Looking up at the man on the stairs, the sheriff recognized Klaw. "Did you see this shoot-out?"

The one-handed man nodded.

"Well, why did this feller kill these men?"

"Self defense," Klaw replied. "Like he said, they drew on him."

"Oh, well," the lawman muttered, hooking his thumbs into his gunbelt. "I reckon there's no need to arrest you then," he told Becker.

"Lucky for you, Sheriff," the former Reb rasped. Becker glanced up the stairs, but Klaw had already disappeared from view.

Chapter Three

∞∞∞∞∞∞∞∞∞∞∞∞∞∞∞∞∞∞∞∞∞∞∞∞∞∞∞∞∞

Major Walter Nelson raised his hand, silently commanding his men to halt. Dressed in a full Army uniform, brass buttons gleaming on his blue tunic, Nelson appeared to be an officer in the United States Cavalry. His companions, however, were an assorted collection of misfits.

A muscular black man, dressed in levis, chukka boots and a denim shirt with the sleeves cut away, urged his gelding forward. He drew a Winchester repeater from its saddle boot.

"Is that the place, Major?" he asked, wiping sweat from his bald head with a palm. He referred to a small farmhouse and barn in the valley below.

"That's right, Big Ned," Nelson replied flatly as he swung down from the saddle, carefully moving the saber scabbard on his left hip. "We'll only need ten men."

"We gonna ride down on 'em or sneak up on

'em?'' Ned asked, jacking a shell into the rifle chamber.

"Why do you think I dismounted?" Nelson asked sharply. He drew a .44 caliber Smith & Wesson revolver and broke it open to check the loads.

"Yes, sir!" the Negro said, throwing an arrogant mock salute at his commander.

Nelson ignored him, aware that Ned despised all whites, even the men he'd allied himself with. The ex-slave wore a four foot length of iron chain around his midriff like a belt, as if he wanted to fuel his hatred and keep it alive. Yet, Ned was reliable. His feelings for the race that once kept him in bondage didn't blind him to the advantages of being a member of Nelson's troops. To be a black man with money is better than being a penniless one.

Chad Summer, a lanky raw-boned man with an unkempt red beard, moved to the major's side. An eight foot long bullwhip was coiled around his neck like a pet blacksnake. Unbuttoning his sheepskin jacket, Summer ran a hand over the walnut grips of a Remington revolver in a cross draw holster. "The sun is just setting, sir," he remarked, his voice flavored with an Alabama drawl. "Maybe we should wait a while."

"I'd think you would have waited long enough, Sergeant," Nelson remarked. "I hope your memory hasn't failed you after more than a decade." His dark green eyes narrowed as he glared at Summer. "I'll be very unhappy if you've made a mistake. The thirty nine other men with us will also be very displeased with you as well."

Summer swallowed nervously. "Don't worry, Major. It'll be there."

"I'm not worried," Nelson replied. "*I* don't have anything to be worried about."

Beside Big Ned was a figure of remarkable contrast to the muscular Negro. Known only as Edgar, he was barely five and a half feet tall. The narrow face under Edgar's black flat-crowned hat presented a ghostly appearance in the dying light. At first glance, Edgar seemed to be an albino, but his pale complexion was artificial, the result of powder and a light touch of rouge to his thin lips. He wore black linen slacks and shirt, with an ornate silver belt buckle in the center of his narrow waist. On each sleeve he wore an ornamental cuff-link with a small silver bell attached. He made no attempts to conceal his homosexuality, and none of the other riders ever mocked him. The slender, soft-spoken Edgar was a cold-blooded killer and an expert marksman with his long barreled Navy Colt cap and ball revolver.

Assembling the men he wanted for the raid, Major Nelson drew his saber. "Everyone knows what he's supposed to do. Let's move."

Alan Corbett's father had settled in Texas before it became a state. A large, rugged man, Corbett appeared to be ten years younger than his forty five years, despite his iron gray hair. The farmer was pleased with his life. He had a loyal, loving wife, three healthy sons and a pretty little daughter. Corbett still enjoyed working in the fields. He was proud of his ability to grow things. When many Texans were leaving to join the Confederacy, Corbett stayed with his farm. He'd rather grow food than kill his fellow man.

He was glad the war had ended. Ronald and Henry, his oldest sons, were both in their late

26

teens. Corbett realized that at least one of his boys—probably Henry—would leave the farm to start his own life and raise his own family. He didn't relish losing his sons, but he'd rather they left to continue the Corbett name than to join the damn armies and their damn wars.

"I heard Old Man Clayton is gonna string up that hunchback blacksmith today," Henry commented, as he shoveled horse dung from the stall of one of the plow horses and dumped it into a bucket.

"You speak respectful of your elders, son," Corbett chided. "*Mister* Clayton has built himself a fine ranch. You'd do well to emulate such a man," the farmer snorted, as he held a horse harness to the kerosene lantern and tried to repair one of the straps. "Since you don't choose to stay here and inherit your father's property."

"Aw, Pa," Henry groaned, leaning on the long handle of his shovel. "I just wanta move into town and be around people."

"You are with people," Corbett told his oldest boy. "Family is the best people a man ever has."

"We've talked about this before, Pa," Henry said. "You say you want'a have grandchildren, and you want us boys to get married and have kids. How can we do that if we stay on the farm the rest of our lives?"

"Don't be disrespectful, boy!" Corbett snapped, immediately regretting his words as he realized his son was right.

"I don't mean to be, Pa," Henry insisted, "but I'd still like to get into Cercano Afeitar. If that Mex hunchback is hanged, then I might be able to get a job as the new blacksmith. I do all right with the forge and anvil here, don't I? I can shoe a

27

horse better than Ron or even you, Pa."

"Maybe you should try it for a while, son," Corbett suggested with a weak grin.

"You mean I can go into town and be the new blacksmith?" the youth asked eagerly.

"Don't get too hopeful, boy," Corbett warned. "Maybe Mister Clayton didn't hang that hunchback today, but if the job is there, you can try to get it."

"Thanks, Pa," Henry beamed.

"Let's get our work finished, son," the farmer advised. "Your mother will have supper ready soon."

"Right, Pa," Henry replied as he turned to shovel the rest of the horse dung.

He froze as he stared into the barrel of a Remington revolver.

"You left the outside door to the stall unlocked," Chad Summer explained, as he pushed by the docile old plow horse and cocked the hammer of his pistol.

"Pa!" Henry rasped, his eyes expanding with fear as Summer drew closer.

"What is it . . .?" Corbett began.

Henry turned to see why his father's sentence had ended abruptly. To his horror, he saw a large black man standing behind Alan Corbett. The farmer's eyes bulged in their sockets as Big Ned tightened the chain wrapped around the senior Corbett's neck. His teeth clenched, Ned pulled harder.

"You left the door to the corral unlocked too," he hissed. "You white boys sure are careless."

Ned raised a knee and smashed it into Corbett's kidney. The farmer's body buckled, his torso swinging sharply as the taut chain kept his neck stationary. Vertebrae crunched. An expression of utter astonishment dominated Corbett's features. Henry watched his father's urine pour down his pants leg. Big Ned unwound the chain from his victim's broken neck. Alan Corbett collapsed to the barn floor like an empty grain sack.

"Pa!" Henry cried, tears forming in his eyes.

Summer slammed the barrel of his revolver sharply behind Henry Corbett's ear. The boy wilted to the floor with a sob. Big Ned smiled as he raised the chain in his big fists and approached the unconscious youth.

"The major wants one of these fellers alive, Ned," Summer urged.

"Damn the major," the black man hissed as he coiled the chain around his waist like a metal belt. "If it weren't for the gold, I'd use this thing on *him*!"

"Better never try," Summer warned.

"The hell with you too, Southern white trash!" Ned spat. "I seen enough of your kind to know you're all loud-mouth sissies. At least Edgar is honest about what he is!"

"You uppity nigger son of a bitch!" Summer snarled, shoving his Remington into its holster and removing the black bullwhip from his neck. "You been away from the lash too long, boy. Time a white man reminded you to keep a respectful tongue in your ape mouth when you're addressing your betters!"

Iron links clattered as Ned unfastened the chain from his waist. Summer dragged his whip along the floor, gaging the distance between himself and his opponent. They drew closer, weapons held ready. As his whip was twice as long as Ned's chain, Summer launched the first attack. His arm

29

snapped out, cracking the twisted leather snake forward in a blur of movement. Ned cried out as the lash struck the side of his neck, tearing flesh painfully.

"Feel familiar, nigger?" the Alabamian sneered, drawing back the whip. "There's plenty more a'coming!"

Ned held up an arm to ward off the next blow, but Summer had selected a new target. Dropping to one knee, he swung his weapon low. The leather curled around the Negro's ankles. Summer pulled the whip with both hands and jerked Ned's feet off the floor. The black man fell heavily with a gasp as his wind was knocked from his lungs.

"You recall what your place is yet, boy?" Summer growled, retracting his whip. "Maybe you're riding with a group of white men, but that don't make you one of us!"

Big Ned rolled over on all fours and tried to scramble to his feet as Summer's whip lashed him across the back savagely. The cloth of the Negro's shirt ripped open and blood trickled from the dark skin.

"You too dumb to learn, darkie?" the Southerner chuckled as he swung his whip again.

Suddenly, Ned's free hand caught the twisted leather lash, pulling it hard. Summer staggered forward, jerked off balance. The black man's chain whirled, the iron links smashing into Summer's ribcage like an alligator's tail. The Alabamian moaned in agony while Ned rose. Fury transformed Ned's ebony features into a dark mask. His muscular left arm lashed out, the big fist crashing into Summer's face, knocking him to the floor.

Ned's chain swooped down, the metal striking

30

Summer's collar bone, almost breaking it. The Southerner tried to get up, but a booted foot launched a powerful kick to his ribs and sent him sprawling across the floor. The black man raised his chain overhead.

"I'm gonna kill you, white trash!" he hissed.

"Stop it!" a voice snapped.

Ned turned to see Ed Sloane, a wiry, black haired man with a pencil-thin mustache. Sloane had formerly served as a sergeant with Major Nelson during the War and currently provided Nelson with a second in command. The black man glared at Sloane angrily, but the Colt revolver in the smaller man's fist prevented him from taking any actions against Sloane.

"This Johnny-Reb peckerwood called me a nigger," Ned explained. "He's gonna pay for that!"

"Not now," Sloane declared. "We're in the middle of an assault, for crissake! This is no time for fighting among ourselves. If you two want to kill each other, you'll wait until we've got the gold."

"If there is any gold," Ned muttered. "This lying hillbilly bastard probably made the whole thing up!"

The whine of hard leather slicing through air filled the Negro's ears a fragment of a second before Summer's whip struck him in the face. Ned cried out, placing a hand to his damaged cheek. He pulled it away and stared at the blood on his palm.

"The gold's there, you shit-colored sub-human!" Chad Summer snarled. "Don't you ever say I'm a liar again or I'll lash your frigging eye-balls out!"

Sloane cocked the hammer of his Colt. "If

either of you make another aggressive movement, I'll kill you both!"

"My face!" Ned wailed, feeling the deep gash in his cheek. "You done scarred my face!"

"You were already ugly," Summer shrugged.

"You're gonna die slow for this!" the Negro vowed.

"The major wouldn't take kindly to you killing the man who knows where the treasure is, Ned," Sloane warned. "You'll just have to wait for your revenge."

"And I sure as hell will!" Ned snarled, stomping to the barn's exit.

Marcia Corbett prepared a beef and potato stew as Annie swept the kitchen floor and ten year old Danny dutifully set the table for supper. The Corbett children accepted their chores without complaining, they were good, reliable and obedient. Marcia was a descendant of Scottish immigrants. A stout, hard-working woman with Old World principles and morality, she had been an ideal bride for Alan Corbett. Life on a farm was all that she had ever known, and it satisfied her to remain ignorant of the alternatives.

"We'll need some firewood," Ronald stated, as he slung an axe over his shoulder. "I won't be gone long, Ma."

Marcia smiled. Ronald was two years younger than Henry, but he was bigger and stronger and healthy as a horse. He always seemed eager to work. Ronald was a born farmer, like his father and his grandfathers on both sides of the family. Henry would probably leave to live in a town—for what reason, Marcia would never understand —but Ronald would remain. The Corbett tradition of farming would continue.

"Go build up a good appetite," she good-naturedly instructed Ronald.

As he reached for the door, it abruptly burst open. Major Walter Nelson lunged through the doorway, his saber in one hand and the S&W revolver in the other. Ronald's astonishment froze his muscles temporarily, but he hesitated less than a second before swinging the axe from his shoulder at the invader. It was the last action of his young life. Nelson dropped into a low fencer's crouch as he thrust the saber forward. Ronald's axe whirled scant inches above the major's head.

The youth screamed as the sword impaled him. Ronald's own forward momentum met Nelson's thrust and helped to drive nearly a foot of sharp steel into his diaphragm. Ronald dropped the axe and staggered backward. Clamping his hands to his mid-section, he stared down at the blood seeping between his fingers. The young Corbett boy crumbled to the floor.

Marcia screamed as she watched the stranger in the blue cavalry uniform murder her son. Why had the soldier attacked them? Was there another war? Where was Alan? Danny and Annie cried out and rushed to their mother's side. Major Nelson moved his bloodied saber across his chest and bowed flamboyantly.

"Good evening, madame," he said. "Sorry to interrupt your dinner plans, but this won't take long."

"What do you want?" Marcia demanded hoarsely, tears streaming from her eyes as she gazed down at Ronald's corpse. Her favorite son had been brutally slain, but the two tiny forms tugging at her skirts urged her to think of her living

33

children instead of her grief.

"An example for the people of Cercano Afeitar," Nelson replied flatly.

The bizarre figure of Edgar entered the farmhouse. His pale impassive features a stark contrast to his black clothing, the gunman resembled a personification of Death. The tiny silver bells at his wrists tinkled as he raised the Navy Colt to his slightly pursed lips.

Edgar's expression remained stoical while he extended his arm, cocked the Colt's hammer and fired. Mrs. Marcia Corbett's head snapped back as the .36 caliber lead ball punched a gory hole between her horrified eyes. The woman fell back onto her stove and toppled the pot. Stew spilled on Mrs. Corbett's splattered blood and brains an instant before her body hit the floor.

"Mama!" Annie Corbett wailed. Her grief was mercifully brief as Edgar's second bullet tore into her forehead and killed her.

Danny Corbett would not be as fortunate.

"You're mine, boy," the powder-faced murderer declared flatly.

Danny knelt between his slain mother and sister, trembling as he wept. Edgar stepped forward, tucking the long barreled revolver into his belt. A bell chimed sharply when the gunman's arm lashed out, the back of his hand cuffing the boy's face hard.

"You're mine," Edgar hissed, gripping Danny's arm roughly. "Come with me."

"Kill him when you're finished," Major Nelson ordered.

Edgar nodded in reply as he dragged the confused and frightened boy into the Corbetts' master bedroom.

A bucket full of dirty water hit Henry Corbett in the face. The youth awoke with a start, shaking his numb bruised head feebly.

"Pa . . ." he moaned weakly.

"He can't hear you, white boy," a voice chuckled.

Henry opened his eyes to stare into the grinning dark face of Big Ned. The youth gasped. As his consciousness returned and his mind cleared, he remembered what had happened before Chad Summer's gun barrel came crashing down on his skull. He slowly became aware of his surroundings. Henry was inside the barn, one wrist was bound to an anvil and the other to the post of a stall. Half a dozen men formed a semi-circle around the boy.

"You killed my father!" he cried hoarsely.

"We killed your entire family," Major Nelson commented flatly. "You've been spared because I want you to go to Cercano Afeitar and deliver a message." The major paced the floor casually as he continued. "You will tell the townsfolk to leave. To encourage them to evacuate, the citizens of Cercano Afeitar will be able to see what we've done here," Nelson shrugged, "and they'll be able to see what we've done to you."

Ned seized the back of the captive boy's shirt tails and ripped the cloth apart. Chad Summer uncoiled his bull-whip as Major Nelson walked from the barn.

Nelson hardly noticed the crack of Summer's lash, followed by Henry Corbett's cries; his thoughts were concentrated on the future and the fortune that awaited him in Cercano Afeitar.

Chapter Four

∞∞∞∞∞∞∞∞∞∞∞∞∞∞∞∞∞∞∞∞∞∞∞∞∞∞∞∞∞

The Barber's Chair Hotel and the Close Shave Saloon belonged to Robert Kehoe, the mayor and founder of Cercano Afeitar. Kehoe, an Irish immigrant, had enjoyed moderate success as a barber in Boston, but the prejudice against his native land was still a constant barrier to his progress. The Molly Maguires, a secret society of Irish-born terrorists among the coal miners of Pennsylvania, had caused a new wave of violence. Many people feared that the large Irish populations in New York and Massachusetts might also contain Molly Maguires or similar dangerous trouble makers.

As Kehoe's business suffered, he began to consider moving West to start a new life. After investigating the various states and territories, Kehoe selected the largest state in the union: Texas. With a handful of fellow settlers—mostly Irish immigrants like himself—Kehoe created the town of

Cercano Afeitar, choosing a Spanish name in hopes of attracting Mexican-Americans to the community.

Klaw wasn't thinking of the history of the town as he eased himself into the tub of hot water in his room at the Barber's Chair Hotel. The luxury of washing in something more comfortable than a cold spring provided him with a rewarding pleasure he hadn't enjoyed since he left Brownsville two months before. Klaw recalled his last day in Brownsville before he rode West. He'd mailed eighteen thousand dollars to his friend, Doctor Melvin Webber in Great Ford, Colorado.

A former captain in the Union Army, Klaw had studied as an apprentice gunsmith after the War Between the States. He'd returned to the town of his birth to investigate the deaths of his parents who were supposedly killed by an Arapahoe raiding party. He discovered that Great Ford had fallen under the absolute rule of a corrupt and powerful banker named Warren Jennings. With a puppet mayor and sheriff, and a small army of gunmen masquerading as bank guards, Jennings' tyranny was virtually unopposed until Klaw launched a one-man-war against the banker.

Klaw sacrificed a great deal to defeat Jennings' totalitarian rule. He became a wanted man and lost his former identity, his right hand and nearly his life in the process. His victory would have been incomplete, however, if he hadn't seen to financial retribution for the people of Great Ford whom the evil banker had victimized.

Doctor Webber had become the temporary mayor of Great Ford, and the town was recovering from Jennings' oppression. Klaw's obligation to his home town was paid. Now he had only himself to think about.

He knew only two trades—the construction and repair of firearms, and how to kill. Klaw's handicap prevented him from handling the intricate tools of a gunsmith. Although he could still handle a gun with the same deadly skill acquired during four years of bloody combat, he wasn't a gunfighter or a hired killer.

Klaw had known he'd need money for his uncertain journey West, but he kept less than one hundred dollars for himself before mailing the rest of the cash to Webber. Had he been foolish to return almost all of the money to the citizens of Great Ford? Perhaps, yet it had been the only action Klaw considered proper. If a man doesn't live by his principles, he'll never be happy living with himself.

Rising from the tub, Klaw toweled himself dry. He examined the stump at the end of his right arm. Skin had grown over the severed limb, and it no longer required bandages or tourniquets. The arm seldom caused any pain since those terrible long months that followed his injury. Adjusting to the sight of his abbreviated forearm had required almost as much effort as learning to cope with the disability itself. Klaw had been revolted by the stump and the blunted scar tissue that formed at the end of his wrist. Now it seemed that the right arm was only a few inches shorter than the left. As Doctor Webber had advised him, Klaw exercised the arm daily to prevent it from withering. He was pleased to see that it was still as well-muscled as his left limb.

Klaw pulled on his levis and denim shirt. Rolling up the right sleeve, he slipped the leather device over his stump, tightening its straps with his teeth.

The inside of the harness was padded for comfort, and the brass base at the end of his arm served as a firm support for the various instruments he attached when needed.

He sat on the edge and opened a cedar container slightly larger than a cigar box. The light from the kerosene lantern reflected on the polished steel hooks. Doctor Webber had purchased the hooks for Klaw. Kindly, noble, Doc Webber and Amos Dunlap, a big-hearted former slave—a blacksmith like the hunchbacked Lazaro—had helped Klaw accept his handicap during those challenging days after the loss of his hand.

He generally wore the large curved hook that served as a grasping tool and, occasionally, a weapon. The other hook was a two pronged contraption that allowed him to use small objects such as a pen. He always kept in touch with Webber by mail and telegram, using the name *K. Johnson*. Klaw could not return to Great Ford, Colorado, and his original name was buried in a rock filled coffin. John Klawson was dead. Only *Klaw* remained.

Klaw prepared to insert the two-prong hook into the end of his arm when there was a knock at the door. He reached into one of his boots by the bedside and extracted a .41 caliber over-under Remington derringer, sliding it under the pillow.

Tom Becker opened the door. The bearded ex-Confederate limped inside and waved a bottle of whiskey. "Figured I'd stop by and thank you for supporting my story 'bout what happened with those bastards in the lobby." Becker closed the door.

"It wasn't much," Klaw shrugged, screwing the two pronged hook into his arm. "I didn't take any

39

risks."

"I still figure I should buy you a drink," he gestured with the bottle. "Hope you like this brand of whiskey. It's all they've got in this horse-dump town."

"No thanks," the one-handed man stated.

Becker's expression hardened. "I take it you're a Northerner. Your accent sounds like you're from Iowa or Kansas."

"Colorado," Klaw told him. "And if you wonder if I served in the Union Army, the answer is yes. I was a cavalry captain. That has nothing to do with why I don't want to have a drink." He held up his stump. "The three fellers that ambushed me a while back and chopped off my hand, also shot me in the gut. I can't handle liquor or even coffee anymore. I'd puke it up a couple minutes after I swallow it."

"You don't mind if I lower the level of this whiskey by myself then?" Becker inquired.

"Help yourself," Klaw assured him.

"I can't help wondering why you didn't tell that fat ass old sheriff that the fellers I killed were bounty hunters," the ex-Confederate mused as he pulled a cork from the bottle. "There's one thousand dollars riding on my head. You sort'a look to me like you could use that kind of money."

"I could use any kind of money," Klaw replied.

"So, I got to thinking that maybe you don't care to draw attention to yourself. After all, Klaw—I got your name and room number from the registry at the front desk—a feller with a missing hand would be pretty easy for some lawman or bounty hunter to spot if he had a reason."

"I'll tell you why I backed your story, Tom," Klaw sighed. "First, the regulators you killed were a pair of vermin that deserved what they got. Second, I'm wanted for murder, robbery and arson, but that's up in Colorado and Kansas, which is too far for any bounty hunters to haul my carcass."

Becker whistled softly. "Robbery, murder and arson, eh? You've been a busy boy."

"But I'm not guilty," Klaw explained. "I killed some men, but they were gunfighters trying to kill me. I stole some money, but I returned it to its rightful owners, And the house I burned belonged to the biggest owl hoot in the West. I figure if I'm innocent, maybe you are too."

"I ain't," Becker grinned impishly. "Maybe you're as pure as you say—unless you just told me a pack of lily white lies—but I'm no crusader or Robin Hood, Mister Klaw."

Becker took a long swallow of whiskey. "After the war, I returned to Georgia to discover the Yankees had destroyed everything I once had. My family was dead, my land belonged to the carpetbaggers, and the blue bellies controlled everything. So, I decided to employ the skills that I'd learned with General Stonewall Jackson and make my living the only way I could. I robbed banks, trains, stage coaches and a couple big fancy homes belonging to carpetbaggers. I've killed a few men in the process, mostly blue belly soldiers and man hunters like those two in the lobby today."

He limped to the single chair in the room and sat down stiffly. "My last big robbery went sour. I was with a gang of train robbers a few months ago. While the rest of the boys gathered up all the valuables from the passengers, Luke Malloy and I went to the Wells Fargo car to help ourselves to the vault. Luke was supposed to be a good powder man. Maybe he was—once. Anyway, something went wrong with the fuse or the blasting cap or . . . hell, I don't know. The dynamite exploded too soon, before we could get off the train. Luke was killed and I . . ." He pulled up his right trouser leg to reveal a carved oak extremity jutting from his riding boot, instead of a flesh and blood calf. "We have more than one thing in common, Klaw. After I was arrested, they amputated my leg at the knee. They didn't want me to die of gangrene before they could hang me."

He took another drink. "Fate is a strange whore. Security in a prison hospital is never very strict, and nobody was worried about a one-legged man running away. If the dumb bastards hadn't fitted me with this wooden leg, I probably couldn't have escaped, but I managed. So, that's my life story."

"You have any special reason for telling it to me, feller?" Klaw inquired.

"I sort of figure I owe you a little something," Becker answered. "Now, seeing as how I got a plan to make some money and I could use a little help, I'm willing to let you in on the deal." He moved the whiskey bottle gently, watching the contents rock back and forth. "The bank in this town doesn't look like much, but I reckon it has enough for two fellers to get by for a while, if we split fifty/fifty."

"No thanks," Klaw replied.

"Hell, you met that cowardly lump, Sheriff Winn," Becker commented. "He's got a couple dumb, spineless pup deputies, but they won't be much of a problem . . ."

"No, Tom," Klaw insisted. "I'm not a bank robber."

"You can learn," Becker shrugged. "Listen, you're a cripple, just like me. Do you figure you're gonna get a job busting bronks or punching cows? You'll be passed up everytime for some dumb son of a bitch with a strong back and *two* hands. That's the way the world is, Klaw. It stinks, but that's the way it is."

"Everything stinks if you're determined to smell something rotten."

"Look at what's left of your arm, damn it!" Becker snarled.

He suddenly pulled his Arkansas Toothpick from its sheath. Klaw leaned back on the bed, his hand sliding toward the derringer concealed beneath the pillow. Becker tossed the knife deftly, catching it by the handle in an overhand grip. His arm swung down sharply, driving the point of the big, double-edged Bowie into his right shin. The knife stuck in his wooden leg as the outlaw glared at Klaw.

"Look at that!" he snapped. "We got a crappy deal from life, Klaw. The world shit on us and it's about time we started shitting on the rest of them in return!"

"The people of Cercano Afeitar didn't ambush me and cut off my hand," Klaw stated. "Three fellers did that, and I've already settled with them. This town isn't responsible for the loss of my hand *or* your leg. I've felt sorry for myself long enough. I plan to make the most out of what I've got left," Klaw narrowed his eyes. "And I'm not a thief."

"All right," Becker nodded. "But you better understand something, Klaw," the ex-Confederate jerked the knife from his wooden leg, "I'm going to rob that bank, with you or without you."

"I don't have any money in it," Klaw replied

mildly as his hand slipped under the pillow.

"Fair enough," the outlaw said, shoving the Arkansas Toothpick into its belt sheath. "Just see to it you don't interfere with my plans."

"Thanks for the visit," Klaw told him.

Becker nodded in reply and moved to the door. Klaw sighed with relief as the outlaw left. He pulled the derringer from under the pillow, grateful that he hadn't had to kill Becker . . . or vice versa.

After writing a letter to Doc Webber, Klaw buckled on his gunbelt and pulled on his boots. He exchanged the two prong contraption for the big hook and attached it to the end of his arm. As a precaution, he donned a corduroy vest and slipped the diminutive Remington into a pocket. He briefly thought of his dwindling financial situation. He had less than thirty dollars left. *The hell with it,* he decided. He left his room and descended the stairs.

The O'Hara Diner was the only restaurant in Cercano Afeitar. Klaw hadn't enjoyed a sit-down supper for months. He'd be on the trail tomorrow, but tonight he was going to eat indoors. Crossing the street, he entered the restaurant. The dining room consisted of several circular tables draped with checkered cloth and surrounded by straight-backed chairs.

Crude paintings of President Washington and President Grant adorned the walls. The stout, pot-bellied Timothy O'Hara hurried to greet Klaw and escorted him to a table.

"We've got some fine chili and tacos," O'Hara advised. "The cook is a Mexican, so he's good at making such things."

44

"Sounds a bit too spicy for my taste," Klaw told him, aware that his fragile stomach couldn't handle saucy foods. "A steak, some unseasoned vegetables and some water would suit me a lot better."

"Water?" O'Hara frowned. "We have beer. Real cold beer. I keep it packed in ice in the cellar."

"No thanks."

"Coffee?"

"Water or milk." Klaw shrugged.

"Milk?" the Irishman's face adopted a confused expression. "I'll see what we can do for you, sir."

O'Hara shook his head as he moved to the kitchen. Klaw casually surveyed the other patrons of the restaurant. They were typical townsfolk, quiet men and women that did their best to make a living at their chosen trade. Their lives revolved around their businesses, their homes and their families. Klaw wondered if he would ever be like them. He shrugged off the notion as O'Hara returned with a pitcher of water and a glass.

"The only milk we had has gone sour," he explained. "Luis isn't accustomed to cooking without using lots of seasoning. He can't promise the meal will be . . . well, outstanding."

"Tell him to do his best," Klaw replied, pouring himself a glass of water. "I'm not hard to please."

"Very well, sir," the Irishman sighed as he returned to the kitchen.

Klaw raised the glass and drank as three men entered the restaurant.

"My God!" a voice exclaimed. "It's Captain Klawson!"

Klaw raised his head to look into the face of his

45

former commanding officer—Major Walter Nelson.

Chapter Five

Klaw had last seen Walter Nelson in the winter of 1864. The War Between the States had continued for three furious, blood-drenched years, and both sides had suffered terrible losses. Despite the Union's superior industrial might, the Confederate forces still fought with determination and zeal. The rebels had gained the upper-hand during the early years of the war, but the tide had turned in favor of the Northern army.

General Meade's army entered the Virginia-Maryland border. Among the troops serving in General McDowell's corps was Captain Nelson. Lieutenant John Klawson had been assigned as the executive officer in Captain Nelson's company. Lt. Klawson personally despised his commanding general. Meade, like General Sherman, had no qualms about making war on civilians. He'd occasionally order the hanging of women and children if he believed they'd helped rebel troops.

General Jeb Stuart had driven Meade out of the Potomac region before. Since, in Klawson's opinion, Meade hadn't improved his strategy, the young lieutenant predicted his side was about to suffer another defeat. Events soon proved Klawson's guess to be correct. General Longstreet, commanding less than a full corps of Confederate soldiers in Stuart's army, clashed with Meade's poorly organized and ill-motivated troops.

Blue uniformed figures toppled from their mounts, and Union soldiers scrambled wildly in all directions. Confederates—some dressed in gray, but most clad in civilian attire—swarmed among the disoriented Yankees. Captain Nelson boldly charged into the rebel raiders. His saber flashed in a series of skillful and savage strokes. Dead and dying Confederates fell to the ground.

Lieutenant Klawson's horse collapsed with two bullets in its side. He drew his .44 Army Colt and fought on foot. General McDowell's revolver misfired as a reb corporal whooped with triumph and charged with a bayonet fixed to his rifle barrel. Before the NCO's lunge met McDowell, Klawson shot the Confederate in the chest and head. He later wondered if he would have saved General Meade under the same circumstances.

Although the Battle of Spotsylvania Courthouse was a humiliating defeat for the North, Nelson and Klawson were recognized for their heroic efforts under fire. Both men received honors, and promotions. They were assigned to different units, neither man knowing if the other had survived the war until that night in Cercano Afeitar.

"Mind if we join you, Captain?" Nelson inquired.

"I've been a civilian for a long time, Major," Klaw replied. "But you're welcome to join me."

Nelson and his men sat down around the table. Klaw considered the pair to be two of the oddest characters he'd ever seen. A massive surly black man with a shaven head and a slender, powder-faced individual who didn't appear to be certain which sex he wanted to be, seemed strange companions for a combat veteran like Walter Nelson. Appearances, however, can be misleading. Klaw cautioned himself not to make any snap judgments.

"Well, Captain," Nelson began, still choosing to use Klaw's former rank. "You and I parted company after Spotsylvania. That was a bad day for the Union, but a good one for us, eh?" The Major smiled. "The army shuffled me to General Meade's advisory staff. I didn't see much action after that. I take it you were in some fighting, however. A pity about your hand."

"I commanded a company of combat troops after Spotsylvania. We had our share of fighting," Klaw answered, "but I didn't lose my hand in the war. That happened about a year ago."

"What brings you to Cercano Afeitar, Captain?" Major Nelson asked. "This place is only fit for animals to shit in."

"My horse wanted to come here," Klaw replied.

Nelson laughed harder than the joke deserved. Edgar smiled, but his expression revealed more desire than mirth as his eyes scanned over Klaw with sensual interest. Big Ned glared at the one-handed man with increased hostility.

49

"Seriously, Captain," Nelson said. "I've got something of a para-military operation in progress. Perhaps you'd be interested in joining us."

"Hell, Major," Ned complained. "This feller only has one hand. He wouldn't be any help. 'Bet he can't even handle a gun worth a damn."

"Captain John Klawson was one of the finest officers and best fighting men that ever served with me during the War Between the States," Nelson snapped, glaring at the black man. "He has acquired more knowledge, skill and combat experience than any two men in our unit, with the sole exception of myself. Such a man—whether he has two hands, one hand or no hands at all—is of more value to us than many of our current members," he smiled coldly as he added, "more than a former field hand, for example."

Ned tensed angrily. The grip on the barrel of his Winchester tightened. "I'll remember that," he snarled.

"See to it, Ned," Nelson replied mildly.

"Your *unit*?" Klaw inquired. "I assume you aren't talking about the United States Army, sir."

"No, I'm no longer in the cavalry," Nelson admitted. "Oh, I still wear the uniform. I earned it. I was a professional soldier before the war, Klawson. I was decorated and praised and commended for my fifteen years of military service—until I was assigned to duty under General George Crook after the war in 1872. That Indian-loving bastard actually charged me with conduct unbecoming an officer. If I'd had the honor of serving under General Sherman, he would have given me a medal for hanging those Cheyenne trouble-makers." He sighed. "Anyway, I was *encouraged* to resign my commission. Apparently,

50

the army doesn't want real soldiers anymore."

"Exactly what sort of para-military operation do you have in mind, Major?" Klaw asked suspiciously.

"Don't tell him too much," Ned warned.

"I'll tell him what I please!" Nelson growled. "The captain and I fought together. I know this man. We can trust him."

"He looks all right to me," Edgar commented, running the tip of his pink tongue along his rouged lips.

Klaw glanced at the homosexual with distaste. "Maybe I'd just as soon not know what you fellers are doing."

"I think you'll be interested," Nelson smiled, "in part of two million dollars."

Klaw's surprise registered on his face.

"During the last year of the war, Confederate President Jefferson Davis realized that the Southern cause was doomed. However, if the bankrupt Confederacy could raise enough money fast enough, they might have been able to prolong the war another year or two and possibly emerge the victor. Davis contacted certain wealthy Texans. As you know, this state was quite sympathetic to the Southern cause. They managed to get every Reb-loving Texan from the richest rancher to the poorest dirt farmer to contribute. Shipping tycoons, politicians, even a certain mining operation in Arizona Territory put in their share. It amounted to nearly two million dollars in gold.

"Jeff Davis was smart enough to realize that such a large sum of gold could not be kept a secret, so he sent a small detail to retrieve the booty—believing a large unit of men would attract too much attention. However, a gang of bandits

51

discovered the gold detail's route and attempted to ambush them. Many of the rebels were killed, but the survivors managed to repel the attackers and escape with the heavy chest containing the treasure. The outlaws pursued them and the two sides clashed in another battle. Although more soldiers died, the rebs again drove back the bandits.

"With only a few Confederate troops remaining, the detail realized that if it continued to be burdened by the gold, the outlaws would overtake them. They had to abandon the fortune or die with it. They chose the only alternative that offered some hope for the Confederacy. The soldiers buried the gold, concealing it well enough to prevent the bandits from finding it, and then they galloped away with the empty chest."

The major leaned back in his chair. "However, the war ended before anyone could report the fate of the gold to Jeff Davis. In fact, only one of the men in the gold detail lived to tell what happened in Texas. Sergeant Chad Summer, fortunately for us, is greedy enough to want the treasure for himself instead of trying to foolishly revive the Confederacy or some other nonsense."

"If he wants it for himself, how does that benefit you, Major?" Klaw inquired.

"Because, last year Summer returned to where they buried the gold. He discovered something that makes claiming the treasure a bit more difficult than he thought it would be."

"They'd buried it in Comanche territory?" Klaw guessed.

"No," Nelson replied. "The town of Cercano Afeitar has been constructed where the gold was buried."

"And we're going to convince these peasants to

52

leave the town so we can do a bit of treasure hunting," Edgar remarked with a coy smile.

"Convince them?" Klaw asked, although he already guessed what they intended to do.

"I have forty men, Captain," Nelson stated. "More than enough to take care of the people in this stupid little town. We'll drive these clods out of Cercano Afeitar or kill every man, woman and child here. We're fighting for more than our country ever gave us . . . two million dollars in gold."

"We already made an example of a farm not far from here," Edgar commented. "We were going to send a farm boy here to show these village idiots that we mean what we say, but that fool Summer killed him with his whip. I suppose the flogging got him too excited and he overdid it."

"All right, soldier boy," Ned snapped. "You know what we're doing, so what do you say?"

"I say you can all go to hell," Klaw replied flatly.

"You'd better reconsider," Nelson warned.

Ned glared at Klaw. "I knew we shouldn't trust him."

Klaw's expression remained impassive.

Edgar licked his lips. "Perhaps I can offer you some special sort of attraction to join us?"

"I don't think so," Klaw declared dryly. "You just stick to your pervert buddies and leave us men alone, feller."

Edgar stiffened. His eyes widened with anger as he slowly rose from his chair. A silver bell chimed gently as he placed a slim hand on the grips of the Navy Colt in his belt.

"Cripple or not," the gunman hissed, his eyes as hard as frozen marble, "no one talks to me like that!''

"No!'' Major Nelson ordered.

Edgar ignored him as he drew the revolver and aimed its muzzle at Klaw. His thumb was still earring back the hammer when Klaw's Remington derringer fired. A .41 caliber bullet slammed into the center of Edgar's powdered forehead. The gunfighter jerked backward from the impact of the slug, his body falling onto a neighboring table. With alarmed cries the customers bolted from their seats, as the corpse collapsed over their dinner plates and coffee cups, dragging them to the floor. Edgar's Colt slid from his limp fingers. A silver bell tinkled a soft dirge.

Nelson and Big Ned also jumped from their chairs. The major's hand hovered briefly over the handle of his saber, then swung to his holstered S&W as Ned moved his rifle to his hip. Klaw cocked the Remington again.

"I've got a round in the other barrel if one of you wants it,'' he declared.

"You shouldn't have done that, Klawson,'' the major said flatly, but he moved his hand from the revolver on his hip.

"It's already done, Major,'' the one-handed man replied, still holding the derringer. "And I'm known as Klaw now.''

"Very well, *Klaw*.'' Nelson hissed the name as if it were profane. "You've crossed me once, but I'm granting you a reprieve for old-time's sake. You won't get another one.''

"Fair enough,'' Klaw nodded.

The major and Big Ned turned and pushed through the startled crowd that had assembled around the scene of the shooting. Horrified, they stared down at Edgar, the bullet hole in his forehead resembling a scarlet spider. The people of Cercano Afeitar were stunned by the killing. Such things simply didn't happen in their town. Their eyes darted at Klaw who remained seated, his diminutive Remington still held ready. They resented him for killing a man in the restaurant—ruining their meal with violence—but the hardness of his flinty gray eyes prevented anyone from criticizing him.

Sheriff Cole Winn waddled into the O'Hara Diner, the Colt Dragoon twitching in his trembling hand as if it was a rattlesnake. Ned and Nelson walked around the fat lawman and moved to the exit behind him.

"All right, everybody," the sheriff declared in a quivering voice. "What happened?"

Suddenly, Nelson spun, his saber clearing its scabbard in a single smooth movement. Cole Winn barely heard the sound of the long blade slicing through air behind him. The sharp edge struck the side of the lawman's neck. Nelson's powerful sword stroke hacked through flesh and bone. Blood bubbled from the stump of Sheriff Winn's neck as his severed head fell to the floor.

Chapter Six

∞∞∞∞∞∞∞∞∞∞∞∞∞∞∞∞∞∞∞∞∞∞∞∞∞∞∞∞∞∞∞

Timothy O'Hara and his customers in the restaurant gasped with disbelief. The hideous, decapitated form of the town lawman staggered forward, then crashed heavily to the floorboards, blood splashing in all directions. The shocking, unexpected violence sapped the spectators of their strength and left them numb with horror. O'Hara's Diner had suddenly become a human slaughterhouse. Even Klaw was startled by the major's sudden and ruthless act of cold-blooded murder. His grip on the derringer tightened, but the finger on the trigger remained steady.

Nelson quickly altered the saber to his left hand as his right whipped the Smith & Wesson from its hip holster. Big Ned raised his Winchester, swinging the muzzle at the stunned onlookers.

"Let this man's death serve as an example to all of you!" the major announced in a loud authoritative voice. "The purpose of examples is to learn from them. If the sheriff isn't enough to teach you to heed my warning, I suggest you all pay the Corbett farm a visit. You'll see that we're prepared to do *anything* to *anyone* to get what we want." He glared at the crowd with contempt. "And we want you to get out of Cercano Afeitar. If any of you are still in town two days from now, you'll die!"

Nelson and Ned backed out the door. "And, Klaw," the major hissed, "the example applies to *you* as well!"

The pair quickly untied their horses from the hitching rail and mounted them. Galloping through the street, the major and Big Ned nearly ran into the bear-like figure of Robert Kehoe as he hurried to the restaurant. A big man with a craggy Irish face topped by an unkept mop of carrot-colored hair, the founder and mayor of Cercano Afeitar nearly stumbled over Cole Winn's headless corpse when he burst into O'Hara's Diner.

"Sweet Jesus!" Kehoe exclaimed, staggering away from the ghastly carcass, his stomach churning. "What happened to the sheriff?" he asked the numb spectators.

"Most of him is right there," Klaw replied as he poured some water into his glass. "The rest probably rolled under a table somewhere."

The mayor glared at Klaw, considering his remarks about the brutal murder of the lawman distasteful and callous. O'Hara shook his head wearily. "Those two fellers that left a minute ago, did it, Bob. The man in the army uniform and the big black buck with him."

"I saw them when I was coming over here to see what the shooting was about," Kehoe declared. He saw Edgar's body and cursed under his breath. "Who the blazes is this, and what happened to him?"

"Some stranger—and—an odd-lookin' one at that," O'Hara replied. "That feller," he pointed at Klaw, as the one-handed man broke open his Remington to replace the spent cartridge before returning it to his vest pocket, "shot him, but the sissy did draw his gun first."

"You again, eh? The man that makes light of somebody killing our sheriff!" The mayor approached Klaw's table.

"He wasn't much of a sheriff," the one-handed man shrugged.

"Cole Winn told me about you and that other feller, that bearded Johnny-Reb that walks with a limp. He figured you two would bring this town nothing but grief," Kehoe said. "And since four men have died in a single day, it appears old Cole was right. May he rest in peace."

"I only killed one man in this town, feller," Klaw stated flatly. "Like O'Hara said, it was self-defense, so get the hell off my back."

The mayor felt a cold eel slink up his spine as he gazed into Klaw's hard gray eyes. He decided he couldn't intimidate the one-handed man, so he turned his vehemence on the rest of the onlookers. "Why did all of you just stand by and watch those bastards kill Sheriff Winn?" he snapped. "Why didn't anyone try to stop them?"

"Probably because none of them were armed," Klaw told him. "From what Winn told me, you folks don't approve of packing guns. If a feller doesn't have a weapon, it's pretty stupid to expect him to go up against somebody that does."

"What's your excuse, mister?" Kehoe growled.

"You've got a gun. Why didn't you do something?"

"All I had was a short-barreled derringer with one shell left. Nelson and his man were better armed than I was," Klaw explained. "I wasn't keen on getting myself killed to avenge the death of your sheriff."

"*Nelson*?" The mayor raised an eyebrow. "You mean you know the man who killed Cole?"

"I knew him once," Klaw nodded. "But the man I met today isn't the officer I served with in the war."

"What does he want?" Kehoe asked.

"He wants this town," Klaw replied simply. "He told everybody in the room that much. I reckon you'd better either give it to him or get ready to fight to keep it," he suggested.

"What would you do?" O'Hara asked Klaw. The mayor glared at the restaurant owner for turning to the arrogant one-handed stranger for advice.

"I'm not you, and this isn't my town," Klaw stated. "What you figure Cercano Afeitar is worth is your business. I only know what I plan to do. I'm going to eat my supper, sleep in a feather bed, and ride on tomorrow."

The next morning, Klaw gathered up his belongings and left his room at the Barber's Chair Hotel. He planned to visit Lazaro Santos at the blacksmith shop and advise him to take Sally Clayton and leave Cercano Afeitar. Perhaps the hunchback and his girl could find a place that would be safe from the twin threats of Clayton's vengeance and Nelson's invasion. Lazaro and Sally were the only people Klaw had encountered whom he considered worth saving. If Lazaro took his advice, the hump-backed blacksmith might survive—if not, Klaw's conscience would rest easy.

As he descended the narrow stairway, the one-handed man discovered a cluster of townsfolk waiting in the lobby. Robert Kehoe and Timothy O'Hara were among the group. The expressions of the six men in the room ranged from hopeful and desperate to surly and disgusted. Kehoe's features displayed all four emotions.

"Since I don't see Sam Clayton among you folks, I reckon this isn't a lynch mob," Klaw remarked, as he licked down a dark-brown cigar. "So what do you want? Most of you are probably glad to see me leave Cercano Afeitar, but I don't figure you plan to stand at the town limits and wave good-bye."

"We had a meeting of the town council," Kehoe announced. "We'd like to talk with you."

"I'm listening," Klaw assured him, striking a sulfur-headed Lucifer match on the railing. He held the flame to his stogie and puffed gently.

"We want to offer you a business proposition," Kehoe explained, the inflection of his voice indicating that he had made the statement with considerable reservations.

"You know what happened last night . . ." O'Hara began.

"Hell, yes! Of course he knows what happened!" Danny Kehoe snorted. A younger, less-flabby version of his father, Danny had followed in Robert Kehoe's footsteps and operated the local barber shop. "You know he was in your restaurant and saw the whole damn thing!"

"I was there too," Millard O'Shea, a frail old man that owned a combination post office and photography shop, stated. "He was sittin' at a table talkin' with the very fellas that killed Cole Winn."

"Friends of yours, Klaw?" Mel Durkan inquired snidely. The manager of the local haberdashery was a beefy, square faced man with a personality as appealing as a gut shot grizzly.

"If they were his friends, they ain't any more," O'Hara declared. "He shot one of them deader than Billy-be-damned!"

"I seen that too," O'Shea agreed. "He shot that funny boy with the painted face right between the eyes, he did. That's some kind of shooting. Just like I used to do when I was a young man, before me eyes went bad."

"What do you folks want?" Klaw insisted, eager to be on his way.

"We need a new sheriff," the mayor explained. "After they saw what happened to Winn, Dave Simpson and Jake Callahan, his deputies, refused to take his place. In fact, they not only won't be the new sheriff, the yellow sons of bitches turned in their badges! They plan to leave town and just let Nelson and his gang swoop down on us."

"That figures from Simpson," O'Shea commented. "But I'm surprised that a good Irish boy like Callahan would run out on us like that. Bet his father was an Orangeman."

"You picked some real fine lawmen," Klaw scoffed as he blew a smoke ring.

"We didn't elect trigger-happy owl hoots like some towns have done!" Kehoe answered sharply. "We wanted somebody to keep the peace, not a gunfighter. Cole Winn was a good man when it came to settling family quarrels and keeping kids from making too much noise on Sundays. Until now, that was usually enough. Oh, once in a while some drovers will come into town for some hell-raising. They might run wild for one night and bust up some property, but we still have our town when the cowpunchers ride on in the morning. If this Nelson fella has his way, we won't have anything at all."

"If you plan to keep your town, you'll have to fight," Klaw warned. "One man won't make any difference if you still act like frightened sheep when the shooting starts."

"The right man could make a difference," Albert Lane, the feed store owner and clerk declared. He seemed embarrassed by his own outburst and began polishing the lenses of his wire-framed glasses. "At least it could, I suppose," he added meekly.

"The man we need has to be good with a gun," O'Hara stated. "And Klaw, here, is about as good as we'll ever find."

"Wait a minute, boys," Durkan urged. "Let's not forget about the other stranger. The bearded feller. Remember, he killed two men yesterday afternoon, right here in this very room!"

"That's right," O'Shea bobbed his turtle-head up and down in agreement. "The fella's name is Tom Becker. The two blackguards already had the drop on him, but, quicker than Saint Patrick can kill a snake, Becker took care of them. He threw a knife into one of 'em, he did. Must handle a knife the way I used to before rheumatism ruined me throwin' arm."

"Seems I recall you were here when it happened, Klaw," Danny Kehoe remarked.

"Well, how about it?" Durkan demanded. "Is this Becker as good with a gun as you are?"

"Maybe," the one-handed man admitted. "I'd just as soon never find out for sure."

"Sort'a sounds like we should hire Becker instead," O'Shea commented.

"No," Mayor Kehoe told them flatly. "Klaw knows the man we're up against. He fought with him during the War Between the States. Isn't that right?"

"Like I told you last night," Klaw replied. "Walter Nelson has changed since we were in the army together ten years ago. The only thing that seems to be the same about him is his skill with a saber. He won honors for his swordsmanship at West Point. Nelson told me once that he'd studied various fencing styles from French, Spanish and Hungarian instructors. I've seen him use a saber in combat. Believe me, last night was no lucky sword stroke." He shrugged, "I can guess what sort of tactics Nelson will use when he attacks the town, but I might guess wrong."

"You're still the best man for the job," Kehoe insisted. "You've implied that we aren't fighters. That's true, Klaw. We founded Cercano Afeitar to avoid oppression and violence. Don't misunderstand us, Klaw, We'll fight if we have to, but we'll need a leader to supervise us."

"So you want me to be your new sheriff?" Klaw mused with a smile.

Kehoe's face screwed up with irritation. "I don't see anything funny about our proposal, Klaw. We'll appoint you to serve as the sheriff of Cercano Afeitar until the crisis is over."

"I'm not amused by the offer, Kehoe," the one-handed man assured him. "But something Sheriff Winn told me now seems a bit ironic. He said if I didn't behave myself I'd be seeing the inside of his jailhouse. Looks like he was right.''

"Then you accept?" O'Hara asked eagerly.

"How much do you plan to pay me?" Klaw inquired as he stepped to the foot of the stairs.

"Since you'll only be on the job for two or three days, we won't give you a regular salary," Kehoe answered. "You'll receive five hundred dollars. That's more than a year's salary under ordinary conditions."

"It's not enough," Klaw told them as he moved among the citizens' committee. "I want ten thousand dollars."

"That's outrageous!" Durkan exclaimed.

"My God," Kehoe said, stunned by the demand. "We're a small town with only a handful of businesses. We aren't rich . . ."

"Yes, you are," Klaw commented with a thin smile. "You just don't know it yet."

Chapter Seven

≈≈≈≈≈≈≈≈≈≈≈≈≈≈≈≈≈≈≈≈≈≈≈≈≈≈≈≈≈≈≈≈

Tom Becker tilted the glass of whiskey to his lips as he watched Julie, Edie and Maria mingle among the customers in the Close Shave Saloon. The girls weren't bad looking for a small, fly-speck of a town like Cercano Afeitar. Julie was an attractive brunette, Edie sported bleach-blonde hair and a full mature figure that would probably run to fat in another year or two, and Maria was a pretty little Mexican who probably wouldn't be eighteen until a couple more birthdays passed.

He slammed the empty glass on the bar. Arnie, the bulky, overweight bartender gestured with a whiskey bottle. Becker nodded. He wondered how much it would cost to sleep with one of the girls for the night. If it wasn't too expensive, he decided to take the Mexican girl. Becker liked young women, the older more experienced females made him nervous.

"Give him the bottle," Klaw told the bartender, placing a silver dollar on the counter.

"Sure thing," Arnie said, exchanging the bottle for the money. "It's seventy-five cents. I'll get your change."

"Don't bother," Klaw replied. "You keep it, feller."

"Thanks, mister!" Arnie exclaimed. He hadn't received a tip in almost six months.

"Why are you feeling so generous, Klaw?" Becker inquired suspiciously, but he picked up the whiskey bottle and pulled out the cork.

"I figure to either acquire a good amount of money soon, or else I won't need it anymore," the one-handed man shrugged. Julie caught his eye as she placed a tray of beer mugs on a table. The girl seemed out of place in the saloon. Her chestnut hair was worn in a casual manner and she wore less make up than the other two women. Although she smiled at the customers, she didn't encourage physical contact. An odd attitude for a saloon girl in a small town like Cercano Afeitar.

"Oh," the outlaw smiled. "You've been thinking about our little conversation, eh?"

"That's right," Klaw nodded. Julie noticed him and smiled, not in a professional manner, but with a wide friendly grin that Klaw found appealing. He tipped his hat politely at her. "Let's talk about it where there aren't so many ears around," Klaw told Becker.

"Good idea," the outlaw agreed.

Klaw kept his right arm low, his forearm hidden from Becker's sight. They pushed through the bat wings of the Close Shave Saloon and walked along the plank walk towards the hotel.

"Generally, when I offer a man an opportunity

66

to work with me on a job, I don't give him a second chance if he refuses," Becker remarked as he took a long swallow of whiskey. "But I'm willing to make an exception in your case."

"I appreciate that," Klaw assured him, leading the outlaw into an alley between the saloon and the general store.

"Do you have all your gear ready to haul your tail out of this town as soon as we rob the bank?" Becker inquired. "I plan to do it this evening around closing time . . ."

"No, Tom," Klaw sighed as he peeled back the lapel of his vest to reveal a badge pinned to the left side of his shirt. "You aren't going to do that."

Becker stared at the copper plated star with disbelief. His left hand nearly dropped the whiskey bottle, but his right fell to the butt of his Tranter. "This had better be a joke."

"It isn't."

"Keep your hand where I can see it!" the outlaw snapped. "I heard how you shot that feller last night with a hide-out derringer." His grip tightened around his holstered revolver.

"Whatever you say," Klaw agreed, swinging his right arm upward. The converted Colt was attached to his stump. His left hand fell to the frame of the weapon, his thumb braced on the hammer.

"Jesus," Becker whispered with astonishment as he stared into the muzzle of the .45 revolver.

"The trigger is wired. All I need to do is cock it and let the hammer fall," Klaw warned. "Before you try any tricks, remember I've seen you in action. I know how handy you are with that Arkansas Toothpick and that little gun at the small of your back. Don't get any ideas about hitting me with that bottle either.''

"You bastard," the outlaw snarled. "So, you decided to take fat old Winn's place and impress this town's dumb mick mayor by catching the notorious Tom Becker, eh?"

"No," the one-handed man replied. "But I guessed what your reaction would be when you saw this badge. I have no intentions of arresting you."

"Then you're either gonna kill me or run me out of town," Becker's eyes narrowed. "You'd better do the former 'cause otherwise I'll be back to settle with you . . ."

"I don't plan to do either," Klaw told him. "I want you to be my new deputy."

Becker's mouth fell open in astonishment. "You're crazy! I'm wanted in four states, for crissake!"

"But not in Texas," Klaw shrugged. "There's no reason you can't be a lawman here."

"Why the hell should I do it, Klaw?" the outlaw demanded. "Did they turn you into some kind of goddamn reformer when they put that tin star on you?"

"Before you decide if you want the job or not . . ."

"You can shove that deputy badge up your ass!"

"Does the idea of a chunk of two million dollars in gold appeal to you more than robbing a chicken-shit bank?" the one-handed man asked.

"Two . . . two million . . ." the outlaw stammered. "Where is it?"

"It's buried here in town."

"So, you aren't a thief," Becker grinned. "Unless the prize is big enough, eh? Well, I don't

68

guess many so-called honest men would stay that way if they got a chance to steal two million in gold.''

"We don't have to steal it," Klaw explained.

"Then how do we get the gold," Becker began, obviously confused. "And how do we keep everybody else in town from finding out about it?"

"They already know."

"But you said . . .''

"I said you'd get a part of two million dollars; I didn't say how many people you'd have to share with.''

"If they know about it, why are they sharing with us?''

"Because I told them about the treasure in the first place," Klaw replied mildly.

"You what!" Becker exclaimed. "Why, you dumb son of a bitch!"

"Now, that's no way to talk to your boss," the one-handed man chuckled, but his thumb remained on the hammer of the converted Colt. "If you want a piece of a two million dollar pie—about ten thousand dollars—you'll have to earn it.''

"By walking around with a stinking badge on?''

"We have to protect Cercano Afeitar from a gang of gunmen that plan to take the town apart in order to claim the gold.''

"How big is this gang?''

"Forty men.''

"Forty!" Becker exclaimed. "This place is full of pepper guts and sissies. Do you think they're going to fight?''

"They'll be apt to do their best for a fortune in gold, and if somebody kicks them in the ass to keep them going.''

"And how are just you and I supposed to accomplish that?"

"You and I and another feller," Klaw replied flatly.

Lazaro Santos hammered a red hot iron into a curved shape. Using his tongs, he lowered the horseshoe into a bucket of water. The metal hissed as it rapidly cooled. He fished it out with the tongs and placed it on an anvil. The sound of a door creaking open drew his attention from the forge.

"Sally," he said as his visitor entered the blacksmith shop, "I told you to go back to your father's ranch."

"I can't leave you, Lazaro," the girl told him. "I love you."

"Do not say that, Sally," the hunchback insisted, staring down at the floor.

"Why? It's the truth." She took one of his large calloused hands in both of hers. "You know it is."

"It will not work for us," he said, shaking his head. "Your father will never approve . . ."

"I'm twenty-one," she stated. "I don't need his approval."

"But you *want* it," Lazaro remarked. "So do I."

"I want you more than I want his blessings."

"Do you want children with crooked spines?" he demanded. "Your father's objection is that this," he touched the hump between his shoulder blades, "may be inherited."

"That's unlikely," Sally replied. "You told me your parents weren't hunchbacked, or your grandparents, or any other members in your family. You just happened to be born the way you are," she smiled, "which suits me just fine."

70

"Unlikely is not impossible," Lazaro told her. "Our children could still be as I am."

"*Anyone* can have children with unusual qualities . . ."

"Deformities," the hunchback stated grimly.

"You're handsome, healthy and strong," she told him. "That disqualifies you from being deformed. Why, your arched back can't even be considered a handicap. You have full use of your hands and limbs—unlike our friend Klaw. You can see, hear and think without any problem. Besides, I'd be proud to have a son *just* like you."

"What about a daughter with a hunched back?" he snapped. "Would she be able to live a full life? I know what childhood is like for a boy with a crooked spine. It would be far worse for a girl."

"We'll love our children, whatever they look like," Sally declared. "Let's not worry about something that probably won't happen."

"If we marry, your father will never forgive you," he told her.

"I have my own life to consider," she said. "I know we'll have to leave this town, perhaps leave the state of Texas, but if that's the way it must be, I can accept that." She cradled his face in her hands gently. "You've given me many arguments to try to turn me away, but only one thing will make me walk out of your life—tell me you don't love me."

"If I were not so selfish, I would tell you exactly that," he said sadly, "but I can't. I do love you, Sally."

Their mouths met. His powerful arms encircled her slender waist in a firm but gentle embrace. Tongues slid into mouths as they kissed harder. Sally's hands caressed Lazaro's humped back as he

71

began kissing her neck passionately. Soon their desire yearned for an outlet.

"Let's make love." Sally urged breathlessly.

"In broad daylight?" he asked, aroused and pleased by her boldness.

"Why not?" she smiled. "Remember the first time we did it?"

"In the hay loft." He nodded fondly.

"It's still up there isn't it?"

"*Si*," he replied. "Waiting for us."

They moved through a door to the livery stable. Climbing the wooden rungs of a ladder, they stepped into the hay loft. Lazaro ducked under the ropes and pulleys that served as a crude crane to haul bales of hay into the loft from wagons below. He pulled the large shutters of the single wide window shut as Sally laid a blanket on the hay covered loft floor. They half stripped and half removed each other's clothing in their haste. Soon naked, Sally sprawled on the blanket. Lazaro gazed down at her body. Her cone-shaped breasts seemed to eagerly await his touch, their brown nipples erect with anticipation.

Sally also scanned her lover's flesh with admiration. His abdomen was encased by ridges of firm muscle. The deltoids and biceps of his shoulders and arms seemed to strain against his dark skin. His hunched back was also layered by cords of muscle. To Sally, his malformed spine only increased his strong masculine appeal. Lazaro lowered himself onto Sally as she wrapped her legs around his hips. They made love for nearly half an hour.

"I must get back to work," Lazaro sighed with regret as he pulled on his trousers.

"Isn't there time to do it once more?" Sally

asked with a disappointed pout.

"I'm afraid not," he replied sadly. "Maybe tonight we can . . ."

He stopped as he saw Sally's eyes widen with fear. He turned to see the source of her terror and faced the muzzle of a Winchester pointed at his broad chest. The loud *click-clack* of the rifle lever sounded like a preamble to Death. Neil Pierce grinned as he raised the barrel slightly.

"I heard you two up here, grunting away like a pair of pigs," the foreman of the Clayton Ranch growled. "So you wanted to get together with your pet hunchback again?"

"Leave Sally alone," Lazaro said flatly as he moved away from the girl. "Your quarrel is with me, Pierce."

"No, Lazaro!" she cried.

"Shut up, you slut!" Pierce snarled. "Maybe I'll never get your old man's spread, but this god-damn freak sure as hell won't be the one to inherit it! Ain't nobody gonna blame me for killin' this humpback-critter. He don't even look human."

"No!" Sally exclaimed as she threw herself at Pierce.

He swung the rifle barrel into her bare breasts, hard steel striking soft flesh cruelly. She whimpered with pain and stumbled to a halt. Pierce removed a hand from the Winchester and swatted the back of his hand across her face, knocking the girl to the floor of the hay loft.

Lazaro's snarl of rage resembled an angry animal's as he charged into the startled foreman. The momentum carried both men hurtling against the window. The shutters burst open. Lazaro and Pierce toppled from the hay loft. The rifle clattered to the ground as the men fell into a pile of hay bales stacked outside the livery stable. The stack tilted over and spilled them to the ground.

Although the hay had broken their fall and neither man was injured, the sudden drop left them winded and disoriented. Pierce scrambled to his feet first and rushed forward as Lazaro tried to rise. A vicious kick to the hunchback's ribs made him groan with pain. Pierce threw a hard left hook to the side of Lazaro's head. His fist seemed to bounce off the blacksmith's skull without effect as Lazaro charged the foreman like an enraged bull. Pierce swung a boot to the hunchback's chest. The blow forced Lazaro's body upright and the foreman knocked him down with a right cross.

Lazaro fell to one knee and tried to rise. Pierce's leg lashed out, his boot slamming into the hunchback's face. Lazaro sprawled on his arched back, blood trickling from his mouth.

"I'm gonna stomp you into the ground, freak!" Pierce announced as he raised a foot over Lazaro's head.

The hunchback's hands flashed and caught the descending boot. He twisted the foot hard, jerking the foreman off balance and sending him abruptly to the ground. Lazaro staggered to his feet, shaking his head to clear it. Pierce rose quickly and threw a handful of dust into the hunchback's face before charging him with a series of vicious punches. Pawing at the dirt in his eyes with one hand, Lazaro tried to ward off the fury of blows with his other arm. Pierce was amazed by the hunchback's ability to absorb punishment, but he knew he'd gotten the upper hand in the fight, and he intended to press his advantage to a victory.

Then Lazaro hit him.

The muscular blacksmith drove a fist into the

foreman's thin mid-section, literally lifting Pierce's feet off the ground. His body involuntarily jack-knifed. Lazaro seized his opponent's shirt front and belt. With a mighty tug, he picked Pierce up and flung him—head over heels—to the ground.

The foreman's back struck the earth with bone-jarring force. Lazaro quickly folded a leg and dropped into his adversary's belly, all his weight concentrated in his bent knee. The foreman tasted bile and lights burst inside his head.

Lazaro's fist smashed into Pierce's face. The hunchback pinned his opponent's arms to the ground with his knees as he struck Pierce again and again. He hammered the bottom of his fist into the foreman's nose and cheek. Bone crunched under the blows. Neil Pierce was unconscious, but Lazaro kept hitting him until a strong hand seized his wrist from behind.

"That's enough," Klaw said.

"He slapped Sally!" Lazaro snarled.

"So hit him one more time," Klaw allowed, "but not in the face. You might kill him."

Lazaro rose, glared down at his vanquished foe and then stamped his bare foot on Pierce's right wrist. Bone grated as the joint disconnected.

"Maybe you picked a good man after all, Klaw," Tom Becker remarked. "I didn't expect a hunchbacked blacksmith to have such a healthy mean streak in him."

"I don't understand," Lazaro admitted. "Who is this man, and what is he talking about?"

"He's the feller you're going to be working with," Klaw replied. "And we want to talk to you about a job."

Chapter Eight

Sally Clayton pulled on her clothes and descended the ladder to join Klaw, Tom Becker and Lazaro in the livery stable where the one-handed man had been explaining why Major Nelson planned to invade Cercano Afeitar.

"So, if we can defend the town, we'll have a fortune in gold to divide among the people of Cercano Afeitar," Klaw concluded.

"Then I must get Sally out of here to some place safe," the hunchback stated with alarm.

"We *both* have to leave town," Sally added, placing a hand on Lazaro's bulging triceps as she dabbed blood from his face.

"Aw, hell," Becker muttered with disgust, "he's yellow after all."

"Here, Tom," Klaw said, handing the former Confederate a cigar.

"Why the stogie?" Becker asked, fishing a

match from his pocket and jerking up his right pant leg.

"Maybe if your mouth is puffing on it, it'll be too busy to say anything stupid."

The outlaw glared at Klaw as he bent and struck the match on his wooden leg.

"Klaw, thank you for the warning," Lazaro told the one-handed man. "You are also leaving town? We can go together."

"I'm staying, Lazaro," Klaw replied as he removed the badge from his shirt and pinned it to his vest. "They made me sheriff."

"But why?" the hunchback frowned. "*Si*, I understand. It is because you need the money."

"That's part of it," Klaw admitted. "But I got a couple of other reasons too. The people in this town want to keep it, and they were willing to stand up to Nelson even before I told them about the gold . . ."

"Wonder if the same feller that carved my wooden leg also made your head," Becker commented sourly.

Klaw ignored him. "A while back I saw what can happen if people aren't willing to fight for what's theirs. There is always somebody who'll try to take what belongs to somebody else. If folks don't stop those kind of vermin, they'll lose more than their money and property. They lose their land, their self-respect and even their freedom." He grimly recalled his home town, Great Ford, Colorado. "Anyway, I decided to help Cercano Afeitar help itself. Also, you and Tom need a chance to start a new life."

Becker snorted. "I never said that."

"If you've got enough money and you change your name, you could live just about anywhere without ever having to rob another bank or hold up another stage coach.''

''Jesus,'' the outlaw moaned. ''You're telling these two all about me! Why don't you put it in the goddamn newspaper while you're at it?''

''Cercano Afeitar doesn't have a newspaper,'' Klaw grinned. ''And don't worry about Lazaro and Sally. They have enough problems of their own.''

''*Si*,'' the hunchback nodded. ''Problems that could be solved with ten thousand dollars.'' He glanced at the girl. ''I wish we could change your father's mind, but I'm afraid that will never happen.''

''But what will Lazaro have to do to earn this money?'' Sally demanded. ''He'd have to stay here and fight, wouldn't he?''

Klaw nodded. ''And the best way for him to do that is to become my deputy.''

''No,'' she objected. ''It's too dangerous. He doesn't know anything about fighting.''

''Tell that to the feller the doctor's putting back together,'' Becker chuckled.

The scent of cigar smoke whetted Klaw's taste buds. He produced another stogie. ''Yeah, Lazaro did pretty well with his fists. Can you handle a gun?''

''*Si*,'' the hunchback nodded. ''I can use a rifle as well as most, but I only own an old single-shot Springfield. I have never fired a handgun, however.''

''We can give you better weapons and the training you'll need,'' Klaw assured him.

''I don't want you to do this, Lazaro,'' Sally urged. ''You don't owe this town anything.''

''But I do,'' he told her. ''*Senor* Kehoe allowed

me to have my blacksmith shop here. For a man with a crooked spine, finding a job is very difficult. The mayor even helped pay for the construction of the forge and provided me with tools, accepting my promise that I would pay him back as the only collateral. Cercano Afeitar accepted me, Sally. For that, I am indebted to this town and *Senor* Kehoe."

"You don't owe them your life," Sally insisted. "There aren't more than fifty people in Cercano Afeitar, including women and children. How can they possibly defend this place from forty professional gunmen?"

"I've got a few ideas about that," Klaw stated, "but the decision is yours, Lazaro. If you accept the job as my deputy, Tom and I will teach you how to stay alive in a fire fight. We've done it ourselves enough times."

"I will stay," Lazaro declared firmly. "You have a deputy, Klaw."

"He has *two* deputies," Becker remarked, shaking his head as he glanced at the badge pinned to his gray tunic. "I can't believe I'm wearing a star."

"You might even get to like it," Klaw grinned as he lit his cigar.

"If you remain in Cercano Afeitar, so do I!" Sally announced.

"No . . ." the hunchback began.

"You feel you owe something to this town," she said. "Well, I feel I owe something to you. I'm staying."

"But Sally . . ."

"My father taught me how to shoot," she told him. "In fact, I'm better with a rifle than you are."

"A lot of women will have to use a gun before this is over," Klaw stated. "We'll find the best cover for the ladies in town. You're welcome to stay, Sally."

"Klaw, she can't. . . ." the hunchback begged.

"Sure, she can," Klaw replied. "And she'll get a share of the treasure as well. Twenty thousand dollars should make a real fine wedding gift for you two."

"I didn't figure you to be a hook-handed cupid," Becker chuckled.

"We all have a little romance in us, Tom," Klaw commented without embarrassment. "You said the world owes us something because we've got physical handicaps. I don't believe that, but I admit we have to try a little harder than most men. I also figure a feller's gotta get a little good luck from time to time, just by the law of averages."

"I've never been very lucky," Becker muttered.

"The best way to get lucky is to make your own luck," Klaw told him.

Neil Pierce stifled a groan. Doctor McParlan, that damn mick butcher, had actually laughed as he dug bits of bone and broken teeth out of the inside of Pierce's mouth. "Maybe that'll be teaching you to leave Lazaro alone," the doctor commented, his Dublin accent as thick as a bison's shoulder. "He minds his own business and I'm glad he kicked your trouble-makin' arse for you!" Some medical man! The Irish son of a bitch shouldn't be allowed to treat horses, let alone people.

Lazaro Santos had inflicted considerable damage. Pierce suffered a broken nose, a cracked cheekbone, a dislocated wrist and the loss of several teeth. His belly felt as if a stampede of longhorns had trampled him. He'd been kicked by ill-tempered mules, thrown by half-wild horses, and he'd fallen down drunk in a campfire and been badly burned, but he'd never hurt so much before. Besides his physical injuries, his pride had endured a two pronged assault. A hunchback—a crippled greaser—had given him the beating of his life, and Sally still rejected him for that Mexican blacksmith with a crooked spine.

What did she see in that goddamn hunchback? Sally was Sam Clayton's daughter, for crissake, she ought to have better sense than to chase after Lazaro Santos. Of course, Sally had guessed correctly about Pierce's interest in the ranch. For ten years he'd worked on the Clayton spread. Since he was eighteen, he dreamed of the day that he'd own a ranch just like it.

When Old Man Clayton's only son, Donald, came back from the War Between the States in a pine box, Pierce could hardly disguise his joy with a false mask of sympathy for Sam's loss. Mrs. Clayton had died giving birth to Sally, and the girl was growing into a fine-looking woman—just the type of woman to be the wife of the new owner of the Clayton Ranch.

Finally, after years of hard work and kissing Old Sam's ass, Neil Pierce had become foreman. Clayton was over sixty and his health was failing. Pierce could see the ranch falling into his hands. Somebody else would be busting his butt in the saddle while Neil Pierce sat in a big armchair, drinking brandy and counting his money. Then Sally fell in love with that damn hunchback, and all of Pierce's plans seemed doomed to failure.

He almost salvaged his dream when he told Sam

Clayton that the hunchback had tried to force himself on Sally. Old Sam didn't need much to convince him. The rancher knew that his daughter had been seeing Lazaro and he didn't like it. If only that one-handed snoop hadn't ruined the hanging. Damn you, Mister One-Hand! Clem Smith and Joe Felder—the ranch hands helping the injured Pierce back to the Clayton spread—had told him that Klaw had been appointed the new sheriff of Cercano Afeitar, and that he'd made Lazaro and some Johnny-Reb with a bad leg, his deputies. The town was becoming a regular freak show!

"Jesus, Mary and Joseph!" Clem exclaimed, pulling back the reins of his mount to come to a halt.

"What is it?" Pierce muttered miserably.

He glanced up and stared at the fifteen gunmen that had emerged from the rock formations on either side of the road. There were too many of them to fight. Pierce tugged his reins sharply, steering his mount to turn around and flee. He froze. Ten more men on horseback waited for them in the rear.

"We're trapped, Neil," Joe Felder said in a trembling voice.

"How'd you guess?" Pierce replied sourly. "Let's hope they just want'a rob us. Maybe we'll come out of this in one piece if we just oblige these fellers."

Major Nelson and Ed Sloane urged their mounts forward, approaching the frightened trio. "Drop your guns," Nelson ordered. Sloane cocked the hammer of the Colt in his fist to accent the command.

"Sure," Pierce nodded, awkwardly sliding his Winchester from its boot and tossing the rifle to the ground. "Whatever you say." He fumbled with his gunbelt with his left hand. His right arm, with its dislocated wrist, was cradled in a sling tied to his neck. Clem and Joe followed the foreman's example.

The major leaned on the horn of his saddle and looked at the three captives with amusement. Big Ned walked to the side of Nelson's mount, working the lever of his Winchester.

"Say your prayers quick," the black man announced. "You ain't got time for no Last Rites!"

"Wait, Ned," Nelson said. "Are you boys from Cercano Afeitar?" he asked the ranch hands.

"No, sir," Pierce replied. "We work for Sam Clayton. He has a big spread about a mile . . ."

"What happened to you?" the major asked, noticing Pierce's battered face, bandaged nose and injured arm.

"The hunchback beat him up," Joe answered.

"Shut up, you idiot!" Pierce snapped.

"Is this hunchback somebody special?" Nelson inquired.

"He's just a blacksmith," Pierce said irritably.

"Not anymore," Joe stated. "Remember? The Klaw made him a deputy . . ."

"Joe, if these guys don't kill you, I will!" Pierce snarled.

"Klaw?" The major raised his eyebrows. "He made a hunchback his deputy, you say?" He smiled coldly. "So the good people of Cercano Afeitar appointed a new sheriff, and Captain Klawson was foolish enough to take the job!"

"Good," Ned commented. "I wanted to kill that bastard the first time I laid eyes on him."

"How many other deputies does Klaw have?"

Major Nelson asked Pierce and his men.

"Just Santos and some drifter that walks with a limp and wears a Confederate jacket." Pierce replied, hoping the information would appease his captors. "They say he's good with a gun and a knife. Killed two fellers yesterday."

"A stinkin' Southern white trash ain't gonna be no problem for us, Major," Ned said as he raised the rifle buttstock to his shoulder. "Looks like these cowpunchers have told us all they know."

"No, Ned," Nelson ordered. "Perhaps, these men can assist us."

"What do you want us to do, sir?" Pierce inquired eagerly.

"Buried in Cercano Afeitar is a fortune in gold," Nelson explained. "We're going to raid the town and claim the treasure. If you'll do us a favor, we'll give you a share of the loot."

"How much loot?" Pierce asked.

"Enough for everyone," Nelson replied flatly. "Now, you have a grudge against this hunchback, and I want Klaw and his deputies out of the way. Maybe you and your boys could take care of them for me?"

"Hot damn!" Pierce smiled. "That'll be a pleasure. I hate that one-handed son of a bitch almost as much as I hate Santos! He killed two of my men yesterday morning."

"Hold on, Neil," Joe urged. "I'd like to have a mess of gold too, but killin' lawmen is like going cougar huntin' with a toothpick. Being rich won't do us no good if we wind up hanging for murderin' Klaw and his men!"

"Who's gonna know we done it, you jackass?" Pierce snapped.

"Joe's got a point, Neil," Clem stated. "We

don't wanta tell any of the other boys at the ranch about this fortune. If we're gonna get them to help us, we can't go back to town and start killing lawmen."

"What do you suggest we do?" Pierce growled.

"What if we just bust 'em up?" Clem replied. "If half a dozen of our men jump Klaw, Santos and the Johnny Reb, we can work them over with pick handles and clubs so they won't be no problem."

"Yeah," Pierce agreed. "If we break their arms and legs they can't be any threat to you, Major!"

"Are you sure you can handle it?" Nelson asked grimly.

"Hell, they're just a bunch of cripples," Pierce replied. "We'll take care of them—especially that hunchbacked bastard."

"All right." Nelson agreed. "Just watch what you say to the men you take with you. If you pay for their services, you'll use your own money to do it." He turned to Ned, "Give them their guns and let them go."

As they watched Pierce, Joe and Clem ride into the distance, Ned shook his head. "You shouldn't have done that, boss," he remarked. "Those cowboys are gonna take a chunk out of all our shares . . ."

"No they won't," the major declared flatly. "After they've done their job for us, we'll cut them out of the deal . . . *permanently!*"

Chapter Nine

∞∞∞∞∞∞∞∞∞∞∞∞∞∞∞∞∞∞∞∞∞∞∞∞∞∞

Twilight descended upon Cercano Afeitar. Klaw, Tom Becker and Lazaro Santos walked through the deserted streets. Only the saloon and the restaurant remained open for business. The lantern light from the two buildings and the bright half moon robbed the darkness of its intensity. The trio entered the sheriff's office.

Klaw struck a match and lit a kerosene lamp. The office was roughly ten by twelve, with scant furniture and no windows. A single, ill-treated and cluttered desk dominated one corner of the room, and a well stocked gun cabinet stood between the desk and a soot-stained pot-bellied stove. A narrow doorway led to the brick jailhouse with its four empty cells.

"We'll take turns making rounds," the one-handed man explained. "Check the doors and make sure everything is locked up. If you see anyone on the streets, make damn sure you know who it is. If you're not sure, challenge them and keep your gun ready."

"I don't think Nelson will send anyone sneaking into town," Becker commented. "Why should he?"

"I can think of two possible reasons," Klaw replied. "The major might want to scout the area to find out what sort of preparations we're making—are we leaving town or defending it? He might send spies in for a more sinister purpose. If somebody burned down a few buildings, it'd be pretty demoralizing. They might even kill a key citizen or two, probably someone like the mayor."

"Or the sheriff," Lazaro said.

"Or his deputies," Becker added. "I see your point, Klaw."

"Fine," the one-handed man nodded as he walked to the gun cabinet. "Now, let's select some weapons for personal use."

"I'm wearing mine," Becker declared, patting the Tranter on his hip.

"You might want a longarm as well."

"I'll take that one," Lazaro said, pointing to a .44-40 Winchester.

"Good choice," Klaw remarked, extracting the rifle from the rack and handing it to Lazaro. "We'll show you how to use it in the morning."

"I have already fired such a gun," the hunchback told him. "Sally and I occasionally go rabbit hunting. She has a Winchester similar to this, but it fires a small caliber. By the way, she *is* a better shot than I am."

"Maybe she ought'a be a deputy too," Becker muttered as he pulled an old brass framed carbine from the rack. "I always favored the Henry repeater to the Winchester for some reason."

"When you figure it out, let us know," Klaw commented dryly. He considered the Winchester to be a far better gun. The one-handed man selected a twelve-gauge, double-barreled Greener.

"Why a shotgun instead of a rifle?" Lazaro asked.

"Working a lever action with this hook is clumsy and slow," Klaw explained while examining the Greener. The weapon was in excellent condition. Someone had sawed the barrels off a couple inches above the forearm grip, but the stock had not been altered. "I also have a hard time trying to squeeze off a shot with this thing," he gestured with the steel extremity at the end of his arm. "But the wide pattern of this shotgun will allow me to hit a target even if I jerk the triggers a bit."

"You won't have much range with that scattergun," Becker warned. "And after two shells, you'll have to reload."

"Yeah," Klaw nodded. "I used a shotgun from time to time in the war. I know its advantages and its drawbacks. In my opinion, the former cancel out the latter."

"Suit yourself," the former Confederate shrugged.

"Time is going to run out fast," Klaw explained as he searched through some drawers and discovered ammunition for rifles, shotguns and revolvers. There were no spare handguns. Simpson and Callahan, the former deputies, had taken their sidearms with them, and one of the good citizens of Cercano Afeitar had helped himself to Sheriff Winn's Dragoon pistol. "We'll have to start fortifying the town to oppose the gang . . ."

A sudden burst of gun fire interrupted his statement. Klaw broke open his shotgun and quickly put two shells into the barrels. He stuffed extra cartridges into his pockets as Lazaro and Becker began feeding ammunition into the magazine slots of their longarms.

"The son of a bitch fooled us all," Becker growled. "He must have decided to launch a night raid to try to frighten everyone into running."

"Maybe we'll throw a scare into his men instead," Klaw commented, cautiously moving to the door and peering outside.

Five men on horseback were in the middle of the street. Their mounts clumped about in awkward circles as the riders whooped and fired sixguns into the air. Klaw frowned. If this was Nelson's idea of terrorist tactics, the major had lost his touch, or he was trying to distract the people of Cercano Afeitar away from a more serious attack being committed elsewhere.

"Ah, that is a relief," the hunchback commented as he peeked outside. "These men have been here before. They are drovers, part of an annual cattle drive from Brownsville to someplace in Nebraska. The drovers aren't supposed to come into town. Sometimes their trail boss arrives and forces them to leave. Otherwise, they will be here all night."

"Kehoe told me about them," Klaw muttered. "They shoot up the place, cause all the damage they want, and everybody is supposed to thank them in the morning because they didn't burn down the town."

"It is not serious," Lazaro remarked.

"It is not going to happen either," Klaw stated.

"You gonna go play sheriff, huh?" Becker

chuckled.

"Yeah," Klaw rasped. "And you're gonna play deputy."

"Why bother?" Becker asked. "Those cow punchers are just going to let off some steam for a while. No sense taking the chance of catching a bullet from one of those drunken drovers. Our real fight is with Nelson's men."

"We're the law in this town, Tom," Klaw told him. "That means we've got a responsibility to protect people's lives and property. Besides, if we let a bunch of liquored up drovers terrorize Cercano Afeitar, do you think the townsfolk will figure we can hold off Nelson? Let's go."

Cursing under his breath, Becker limped to the door. The drovers awkwardly dismounted and tied the reins of their horses to the hitching rail in front of the saloon. Stumbling drunkenly, they staggered through the batwings as the lawmen stepped onto the plank walk.

"How'd they get drunk so soon?" Becker mused. "They must have gotten liquor before they rode into town."

"Sometimes a trail boss will give his men enough whiskey to get good and drunk if they promise not to go into town," Klaw explained. "That way they raise hell in camp instead of upsetting the local population. Sometimes it works, sometimes it doesn't."

"Well, it didn't this time," Becker said sourly. "How do you want to handle this?"

"You two know where the side door to the saloon is," Klaw answered. "You'll both enter through it. It'll probably be unlocked, but break it in if you have to."

"I reckon you're going through the front,"

Becker commented.

Klaw nodded.

"Hope those good old boys don't blast you back through the batwings the minute they see that star on your chest."

"Me too," the one-handed man replied as they walked across the street to the Close Shave Saloon.

Delbert Laird reached across the counter and seized Arnie by the shirt front. The drover snarled at the bartender, revealing large square teeth stained by chewing tobacco. Arnie's nostrils recoiled from the stench of Laird's body odor and the heavy smell of cheap whiskey on his breath.

"What do you mean you can't give us no credit?" the ill-tempered drover demanded. "My friends and I came here to have a good time. Why don't you want us to have a good time, mister?"

"It's just . . ." Arnie stammered. "It's just that we operate on a cash-only system and . . ."

Laird shoved the bartender hard. Arnie crashed into a stack of shot glasses and beer mugs, sending them shattering to the floor. "You're just plain nasty, feller," the drover declared. "Seems we need a new bartender or two." He turned to his men, "Chris! Art!"

Two equally grimy drovers climbed over the bar with a cry of glee. They picked up the protesting Arnie and hurled him over the counter. The bartender hit the floor hard as Julie rushed to help him. Other patrons in the saloon recoiled from the remaining pair of drovers who sat down at separate tables and urged their friends behind the bar to throw them bottles. Chris and Art happily obliged, pitching whiskey bottles at their mates who awkwardly tried to catch the projectiles, laughing drunkenly when they missed and a bottle shattered on the floor.

"Hold on, sweetie," Laird said, catching Julie by the wrist. He pulled her from Arnie's side, his rank breath assaulting her face. "He ain't in no condition to handle a woman, but I sure am."

"Please, let go of me," she replied, trying to be polite.

"Too good for me, huh?" Laird growled.

"Hey, Del," one of the drovers urged. "Take it easy."

"Shut up!" Laird snapped. "This two-bit saloon floozy thinks she can treat me like dirt, and you tell me to just let her get away with it?"

He swung Julie around by her captive wrist and slapped her across the face with an open palm. "Cheap whore!" The back of his hand cracked against the other side of her face. Julie cried out as the blow rocked her head forcibly to one side.

"Hit her again and you're dead!" Klaw declared as he pushed through the batwings.

The drovers reached clumsily for their holstered sidearms, but froze as they saw the big, side-by-side Greener in Klaw's hand. He braced the shotgun against his hip as he curled a finger around the first trigger.

"Anybody who tries to go for his gun will be splattered all over the walls," the one-handed man warned.

"Who the hell are you?" Laird asked, releasing Julie. "You the sheriff? I thought fat old Cole Winn was the sheriff."

"I'm the feller who's ready to kill you if you blink an eye wrong," Klaw replied flatly.

"You figure you can get all of us with that scattergun?'' Laird asked, trying to conceal his fear as the twin muzzles faced him.

"I figure after the rest of these boys see what a blast of buckshot does to you, they won't be too eager to be next," the one-handed man told him.

One of the drovers behind the bar seized a bottle by its neck and prepared to throw it at Klaw. A low whistle drew his attention, and he turned to see the muzzle of a Henry carbine aimed at his head.

"It's lousy whiskey," Becker said, "but it's all we've got. Put it down and climb over the bar. Both of you."

The drovers stared at the rifles in Lazaro and Becker's hands as the deputies moved into the saloon. Chris and Art docilely climbed from behind the bar as the others raised their hands.

"Get them all to one side of the room," Klaw instructed.

Becker and Lazaro herded the drovers away from the bar, but Klaw lowered his shotgun barrels to block Delbert Laird's progress. "Not you," he hissed. "Bastards that beat up women don't get off with just a warning!"

Seeing the cold, controlled fury in the one-handed man's gray eyes, Laird decided Klaw was about to kill him. He realized he couldn't draw his Colt before the sheriff used the shotgun. Desperately, Laird grabbed the Greener's twin barrels with one hand and pushed them toward the ceiling. He reached for his sidearm with the other hand. Maybe the two deputies would gun him down, but he was going to take this hook-handed sheriff to the grave with him!

Suddenly, Klaw's right arm slashed out. The point of the steel hook stabbed into the flesh under Laird's chin. Klaw pulled savagely to one side. The hinges of Laird's jaw cracked, and skin under his cheek bones ripped. Blood gushed over the drover's shirt as he staggered backward. Onlookers gasped in horror when they saw Laird's face—what was left of it. His features ended at his upper jaw, the single row of tobacco stained teeth splashed with crimson droplets.

Laird crumbled to the floor. The other drovers trembled as the hard-eyed Klaw turned to face them. "Now, the rest of you fellers will get the hell out of town," he told them. "And if you ever come back, you'll conduct yourselves in a civilized manner, or you'll end up like your friend here."

Even Tom Becker was startled by Klaw's actions, but he didn't reveal his emotions as he spoke. "You fellers understand?" he asked the drovers.

They nodded woodenly.

"Take him with you," Klaw ordered, indicating the mutilated figure of Laird, curled up on the sawdust floor. "He'll probably be dead in a couple hours, so you can bury him somewhere outside of town."

The drovers were horrified, but they again nodded in agreement. Klaw stepped away and casually kicked Delbert Laird's blood-laced severed jawbone across the floor.

Chapter Ten

~~~~~~

After the drovers departed, Klaw and his men divided the rounds into individual shifts: Klaw would take the seven to nine watch that night; Becker's first guard duty would be nine to eleven; Lazaro would have eleven to one a.m.; then Klaw and Becker would have two more shifts until dawn.

Klaw's thoughts wandered as he walked his first watch, his shotgun tucked under one arm. He recalled the Walter Nelson that he'd known during the war. Captain Nelson had been a good soldier, willing to follow orders and charging bravely into battle without regard for personal risk. He also had had limited regard for the lives of his men, and he never expressed any political or moral views concerning the war. Klaw now realized that Nelson had only cared about his own military career. The war had offered a chance to make some fast promotions. To Captain Nelson, everything else had been secondary.

Memories aren't worth horse dung if they don't help you in the present, Klaw thought. How will Nelson attack Cercano Afeitar? Despite what he'd told Becker, Klaw didn't think Nelson would send anyone into town under cover of darkness. Nelson had always regarded spies as a contemptible and unreliable breed of men. He had opposed their use in the War Between the States because he felt an agent would be too likely to be discovered by the enemy and captured. A spy, in Nelson's opinion, was a weakling and a coward who would be apt to tell his captors valuable information or even defect to the enemy camp. Yet, Major Nelson had changed since 1864. The lawmen would still walk their watches in case Nelson had acquired some respect for surreptitious tactics.

What had been Nelson's tactics in the past? Klaw recalled that his former commander had never been a strategist. Nelson was a strict disciplinarian and a good fighter, but he'd never impressed Klaw with his ability to plan a battle or position his forces to their best advantage.

Klaw smiled thinly as he remembered the nights in camp when he and Nelson had set up a chessboard. Nelson had been a lousy chess player. He had too eagerly put his bishops, rooks and queen into the battle, hoping to checkmate his opponent quickly by the force of his most powerful pieces. Lieutenant Klawson would form a strong defense, allow Nelson to move his men forward and capture them one by one. Captain Nelson had never won a chess game against his executive officer.

A frontal attack—ruthless, bold and daring —was Nelson's style. That is, if the major hadn't *changed* his style over the years. Suddenly he heard the sound of wood creaking underfoot. He whirled sharply, the shotgun braced at his hip, the hook inserted into the trigger guard. Julie gasped as she stood on a flight of wooden stairs in an alley between the saloon and the barbershop.

"Good evening, sheriff," she said in an unsteady voice.

"It almost got ruined by a nasty accident," Klaw remarked, lowering his Greener. "Now isn't a good time to be going for a stroll, ma'am."

"I'm not going anywhere," Julie replied, descending the stairs. "I saw you from my window. I wanted to thank you."

"Looking after folks is my job, ma'am," he told her, noticing how the moonlight accented the features on her pretty face.

"Please call me Julie."

"Certainly," he smiled.

"I've been working in places like this for almost six years," she began. "Most men don't care what happens to a girl they . . . meet in a saloon. No one ever defended my honor before." She laughed bitterly.

"Everybody's got some honor, Julie," Klaw told her.

"Well, I've kept a few principles," she stated. "I never sleep with a man just for money." She drew closer. "If I like somebody enough, I'll give myself freely."

"Like anybody lately?" Klaw inquired.

Julie smiled. "Come with me."

She mounted the wooden steps leading to her room above the Close Shave Saloon. Klaw followed her.

Mel Durkan, the owner of the local haberdashery, tightened his grip on the frame of his Spencer rifle, trying to keep his hands from shaking. Luis Gonzales, the pot-bellied cook from the O'Hara Diner, held a shovel in his sweaty hands. Dave Simpson, a tall lean young man with a wedge-shaped face, checked the loads in his .44 Colt revolver. Durkan opened the side door of his store and stepped into the alley, followed by Luis and Simpson. If they'd emerged from the alley a minute earlier, they would have encountered Klaw.

"You'd better be right about this, Durkan," Simpson whispered harshly. "This town isn't gonna be too happy to see me again after me and Callahan quit when the sheriff got killed."

"I tell you the ground was lumpy and uneven. Grass grew everywhere else around here except there," the Irishman replied. "It has to be where the gold is buried."

"I hope you remembered the location correctly, *senor*," Luis remarked grimly. "I think it would not be good if we broke into the feed store for nothing."

"And I think you're bloody lucky I chose you to help me, Gonzales!" Durkan hissed.

"All right," Simpson rasped. "We know why you let us in on the deal, Durkan. You needed somebody that didn't have a wife or kids so we can haul ass out of town without taking a bunch of people and belongings with us and attracting the whole damn town's attention. You also had to have a couple fellers that had no love for Cercano Afeitar. Me and Luis fit both categories, so let's get to work so we can get the gold and leave."

The trio scrambled across the street to the livery stable. Durkan and Luis panted heavily as they reached the building. The young and slender Simpson glared at his overweight companions with disgust. The three men moved to the rear entrance of the feed store. Luis aimed the blade of his shovel at the door jamb and put all his two hundred and fifty pounds into an awkward but powerful charge. Metal struck wood with a sharp *crack* and the door lock burst open from the impact. The trio quickly entered the unlit feed store and closed the broken door.

"Christ," Simpson muttered. "Did you have to make so much noise?"

"No need to worry," Luis assured him. "Albert Lane owns this place, but he usually stays at the hotel after closing hours. Lazaro the hunchback is now a deputy, so he no longer sleeps in his blacksmith shop."

"That cripple a deputy?" Simpson shook his head with disbelief. "It's plum crazy."

"We'll have to tear up the floor boards," Durkan whispered. "Let's start over there." He pointed to a corner by the west wall.

"We'll probably have to tear the whole place apart before we find it," Simpson growled. "If the damn treasure isn't . . ."

The sound of a man stumbling in the darkness terminated his sentence. Clad only in a nightshirt, Albert Lane strained his myopic eyes to try to see the intruders lurking in the unlit room.

"Who's there," he croaked fearfully. "What do you want?"

He rubbed his glasses on his nightshirt and raised them to his face. Durkan saw the reflection of light on one of the lenses and mistakenly believed it to be the glint of a gun barrel. The Irishman swung his Spencer toward the ghostly form in the white nightshirt and pulled the trigger. The roar of the big rifle seemed to rattle the building. A .52 caliber bullet crashed into Albert Lane's narrow chest. His frail body hurtled to the floor.

Lazaro Santos had returned to the blacksmith shop to collect his clothing and shaving gear. He was startled by the explosive shot in the nearby feed store. Quickly, the hunchback gathered up his Winchester and hurried to investigate the incident.

"You idiot!" Simpson snapped, his ears still ringing from the sound of the Spencer. "We've gotta get out of here now!"

"I had to do it . . ." Durkan whined.

"*Si*," Luis commented sarcastically. "He was about to shoot you with his glasses."

"Come on," Simpson insisted. "Let's move!"

The click-clack of a rifle lever arrested their attention.

"Stop right there!" Lazaro shouted, as he pushed the rear door open and thrust the Winchester into the dark feed store.

"Don't shoot!" Durkan cried, dropping the Spencer to raise his hands overhead.

"Simpson!" Lazaro exclaimed, recognizing the former deputy even in the poor light inside the room. "So you decided to return to Cercano Afeitar. Keep your hands where I can see them."

The renegade lawman obeyed the hunchback's order. He struggled to keep his eyes away from Luis Gonzales who stood unnoticed by Lazaro in the shadows. "Listen, Santos," Simpson began. "We know where the gold is. Let's make a deal . . ."

"Don't insult me by such a suggestion," the hunchback spat. "You know where the jail is. This

100

is where we are going . . ."

Suddenly, a shovel lashed out at Lazaro. It struck the Winchester, ripping it from Lazaro's grasp. Luis swung the tool again. Lazaro dodged the descending blade of the shovel. The thick shaft struck the hunchback's well-muscled shoulder, wood snapping under the force of the blow. Lazaro fell stunned to the floor. Durkan retrieved his Spencer rifle and Simpson drew his Colt. Both men aimed their weapons at the dazed deputy.

"Well, Durkan," Simpson growled. "You got us into this mess, you kill him."

"I . . . I . . ." the Irishman stammered.

"Kill him!" Simpson snarled.

Lazaro stared up at his assailants, more angered and embarrassed by his mistake than afraid of the violent death about to claim him. Durkan jacked a round into the breech of his Spencer and lowered the enormous muzzle.

"Ahhhwww!" the Irishman screamed as he jerked backward. He pulled the trigger of his rifle and fired a big .52 bullet harmlessly into a wall. The Spencer fell from his fingers as he tried to reach the source of his agony between his shoulder blades. The Irishman sank to his knees. Simpson and Luis saw the handle of an Arkansas Toothpick in Mel Durkan's back. More than half of the fourteen inch blade was buried in his spine. Durkan sprawled on his belly and died.

Simpson leaped into the shadows and fired a hasty shot at the figure of Tom Becker who hurtled through the open feed door, diving for cover behind a pile of grain sacks. Becker dragged his Tranter from its holster as Luis scooped up the discarded Spencer. The Mexican cook was still cocking the rifle lever when Becker's revolver boomed. A .45 caliber slug smashed into Luis Gonzales' face.

Dave Simpson thumbed back the hammer of his .44 as he tried to locate Becker by the Tranter's muzzle flash. He snapped off a shot, the bullet tearing into the sacks of grain where Becker had been. However, the former Confederate had already changed his position and fired back at Simpson from the cover of the clerk's counter. The .45 round chewed wood from a support post near Simpson's face. The renegade recoiled and cocked the hammer of his Colt.

Two strong hands seized the former deputy's wrist without warning. Lazaro Santos twisted the captive arm hard, forcing Simpson's hand to open. The .44 fell to the floor. The powerful hunchback then closed one hand around Simpson's throat and grabbed his belt with the other. He lifted the startled renegade off the floor and hurled him forcibly into the nearest wall. Dave Simpson's head and shoulders smacked into the unyielding wood. He slumped to the floor in an unconscious heap.

"You all right, Lazaro?" Becker called. He advanced slowly, his Tranter revolver still ready in his hand.

"*Si*," the hunchback replied. "I thought my shoulder was injured but it is nothing."

Klaw appeared in the doorway, the shotgun in his left hand as he held up his trousers with the hook at the end of his arm. Becker snorted with disgust.

"Where the hell were you, sheriff?" he asked.

"I . . ." Klaw shrugged, trying to conceal his embarrassment. "I was a little preoccupied."

Chapter Eleven

The gun shots aroused the people of Cercano Afeitar. Soon, most of the population had gathered in front of the feed store. Klaw, Lazaro and Tom Becker stood on the plank walk with their half-conscious prisoner and explained the incident to the crowd.

"So you folks go back to bed," Klaw told them, although he knew they wouldn't disperse easily.

"That's Dave Simpson," Timothy O'Hara cried, pointing at the renegade lawman wedged between Lazaro and Becker. "That misbegotten son of a banshee wasn't willing to help us defend the town, but he didn't mind coming back to cause trouble!"

"And he didn't object to killing Albert Lane," Danny Kehoe remarked grimly.

A murmuring of angry voices swarmed the assembly like a threatening hive of wasps.

"I didn't kill him," Simpson shouted. "Durkan shot Lane, not me!"

"But he's already dead, so we can't hang him," Becker commented.

"Watch it, Tom," Klaw warned in a whispered tone. "These folks are mighty upset. We might have a lynch mob on our hands if we aren't careful."

"Lynch mob," Simpson rasped, his eyes wide with fear. "No! You can't let them hang me!"

"Shut up!" Klaw hissed.

Simpson did exactly the opposite—he raised his voice to a near-scream as he addressed the crowd. "I know where the gold is! We can all share the treasure right now!"

Another murmur, this time flavored with eager curiosity as well as anger, buzzed through the crowd. "But you were going to claim it for yourself, you murdering bastard coward," O'Hara snarled. "I don't know how you got Luis to join you in this foul business, but you deserve to hang for that reason alone."

"Wait a minute," Arnie the bartender said. "Why shouldn't we listen to Simpson? If he knows where the gold is, we can dig it up now and high tail it out of town before this Major Nelson can swoop down on us like a goddamn vulture. Why get a bunch of people killed, if we can all be rich without any more bloodshed?"

"My father practically built this town single handed," Danny declared. "And now you all plan to run out on him when Cercano Afeitar is in trouble! Damn the lot of you! You must have English blood in your veins!"

"No need to use such language, Danny," Doctor McParlan remarked. "One fella suggestin' we get the gold and run isn't the whole bloody town.''

"But why shouldn't we do exactly that?" Doris Barrow, the wife of the hotel desk clerk, demanded. She was a big, strong-willed woman in contrast to her waspy and timid husband. "Didn't we come to Cercano Afeitar to avoid the trouble and violence that plagued us up North? Does it make sense for us to fight now? To engage in exactly the kind of blood letting we came here to escape?''

"You and your yellow-bellied husband go ahead and leave," Danny Kehoe snarled. "We can get along without the likes of you. This is our town, and no one is going to drive us out of it.''

"What about your wives and children?" Arnie asked, a touch of desperation in his voice. "Doesn't anyone care what happens to them?''

"I care about what happens to that turn-coat Simpson," O'Hara bellowed. "We can't let him get away with this!''

"Yeah, he tried to get all the gold for himself!" a voice shouted.

"Our families! We have to think of our families first!" another cried.

"String the bastard up!''

"Tear down the feed store and get the gold! Albert's dead, it won't do him no good now!''

"Get a rope!''

The citizens of Cercano Afeitar were emotionally divided. Some were eager to find the treasure and flee, others wanted to lynch Simpson, and a few were in favor of both. Klaw decided it was time to take command of the situation. He took his Remington derringer from its vest pocket and fired a shot into the air. Everyone fell silent, startled by the unexpected blast.

"Now that I have your attention," Klaw announced, putting the derringer away, "listen carefully. You folks appointed me your sheriff, and I plan to do what's best for everyone in Cercano Afeitar. Anybody who wants to leave can do so, but they'll say good-bye to their share of the gold if they do. Nobody is going to tear down the feed store or anything else in this town—until Major Nelson is no longer a threat."

"This is our town, Klaw," a voice shouted. "Who are you to tell us what we can or can't do?"

"I'm just your sheriff," the one-handed man admitted. "But I'm also the only person that isn't talking like an hysterical jackass. We don't have any proof that the treasure is buried under the feed store. That was just a crazy notion Durkan came up with. We don't have time to take this town apart and dig for the gold. Major Nelson isn't going to give us much time. We've got to concentrate on getting this place ready to defend against Nelson."

"But if the gold is buried under the feed store . . ." Arnie began.

"Then what?" Klaw demanded. "You folks think you can find the gold, gather up your families and your belongings, and get far enough from Cercano Afeitar that Nelson can't track you down? How long do you think it'll take him to realize the gold is gone and which way you went with it?"

The crowd remained silent.

"You've only got two choices," Klaw told them. "You'll stay here and fight, or you'll run like spooked cattle. Make up your minds."

"What about Simpson?" O'Hara demanded.

"What do you plan to do with him?"

"I won't stand for any lynchings in my town!" Robert Kehoe declared.

"The mayor's right," Klaw added. "We'll put Simpson in jail until the circuit judge arrives. He'll get a legal trial and . . ."

"Let's give him a trial right here and now!" O'Hara shouted. "He's guilty and we all know it!" Several other voices cried out in agreement.

"There's plenty of evidence to get Simpson convicted," Klaw said. "You folks will just have to wait for his hanging. You'll probably get your belly-full of killing in the next two days anyway."

Finally, the crowd began to dissolve. The people of Cercano Afeitar eventually returned to their homes and beds, but few of them would sleep that night. They'd nearly been part of a lynch mob, and their lack of control frightened them.

Klaw completed his rounds at nine o'clock. He returned to the sheriff's office and Tom Becker assumed guard duty.

"Glad to see you didn't get *distracted* again," Becker remarked, canting the Henry carbine to his shoulder.

"Pay special attention to the feed store," Klaw told him, trying to ignore the deputy's barb. "Some more people might try a little moonlight treasure hunting." He smiled weakly, "And try to stay more alert than I did earlier tonight."

"Don't worry," Becker chuckled. "That little Mex gal is more my type anyway."

He limped out of the office and closed the door. Klaw clucked his tongue with irritation. His unscheduled encounter with Julie could have had far worse consequences. Becker had a right to rub Klaw's nose in his mistake.

Lazaro Santos sat at the desk cleaning and oiling his disassembled Winchester. He looked up and nodded at Klaw as the one-handed man fastened his hook to the back rest of a chair and dragged it into the jail section. Towing the furniture into a vacant cell, Klaw placed his shotgun on the floor near the cot and unbuckled his gunbelt.

"Klaw," Dave Simpson called softly from a neighboring cell.

"Yeah," the one-handed man replied as he placed the gunbelt on the seat of the chair.

Simpson stood by the door of his cell, his fists balled around the iron bars. "The gold might be where Durkan said . . ."

"Right now, I don't really give a damn," Klaw told the prisoner. He hung his vest on the back rest and sat on the cot to remove the steel hook from the end of his arm.

"We can split the fortune," Simpson declared. "Fifty-fifty."

"You know something, Simpson," Klaw began, unfastening the leather sleeve from his stump. "I'm trying to get some sleep. So why don't you just shut up before I decide to shoot you in your oversized mouth?" Klaw stretched out on the cot and yawned. "Or maybe I'll toss you to the people of Cercano Afeitar and tell them to do whatever they want with you. Robbing and killing is one thing, but keeping a feller from getting his sleep is too much for any man to put up with."

Klaw pulled the brim of his stetson over his eyes. Simpson didn't utter another word the rest of the night.

After Tom Becker and Lazaro Santos finished their rounds, Klaw walked another shift without further incident. He returned to the cell for a short nap and was awakened when Becker entered another cell and flopped down on a cot.

"Last watch?" Klaw asked, his voice distorted by the hat over his face.

"Yeah," the deputy replied with a weary sigh. "It's dawn, if you want to go greet the sun or something."

"I've got a lot to do today," the one-handed man muttered as he sat up and slipped the leather sleeve over his stump. "I may as well get started now."

Becker grunted in reply. Klaw inserted the hook into the brass base at the end of his arm and walked from the cell. The scent of freshly brewed coffee tugged at his nostrils. The smell stirred memories of days when Klaw started his mornings with a cup of hot black coffee. Those days were gone, destroyed by a small caliber bullet in the gut. Klaw had adjusted to the loss of his hand and abstaining from whiskey for the rest of his life, but he still yearned for a cup of coffee.

"*Buenos dias*," Lazaro greeted as he poured some coffee into a tin cup. "How are you this morning?"

"Wishing I had somebody else's stomach," Klaw muttered as he ladled some water from a bucket.

"It is well water," the hunchback explained, sipping from his cup. "I got it to make the coffee."

"I noticed," Klaw commented, watching with envy as his deputy consumed the hot black liquid.

"There is another cup if you . . ."

Before Klaw could refuse the offer, the door was flung open without warning. Neil Pierce and five

109

other men squeezed into the office rapidly. Lazaro dropped his coffee cup and moved towards his Winchester by the desk.

"Hold it," Pierce ordered, aiming his .44 Colt at the hunchback. "Leave the gun and get over here."

Klaw cursed himself for leaving his weapons in the cell. He noticed the five men with the foreman were armed with axe handles and short clubs, but only Pierce carried a gun. He guessed the intruders' intentions before the ringleader spoke again.

"We're gonna give you cripples the beating of your lives," Pierce declared. "You're gonna be flat on your back for a year, Klaw, if you live that long." His mouth twisted into a vicious smile. "And you ain't gonna be a hunchback no more, Lazaro, 'cause we're gonna bust your spine in two!"

"Wait a minute, Pierce," Klaw urged, hoping that Becker could hear their voices and would come to their aid. "Let's make a deal."

"You ain't got nothing to deal with, Mister One-Hand," the foreman chuckled.

"Are you sure of that?" Klaw inquired.

"Even if you did have something," Clem Smith stated, "we ain't interested."

Tom Becker limped into the office, unarmed with his hands raised overhead. "One of these sons of bitches is still outside," the disgruntled deputy explained. "He poked a rifle barrel between the bars of the cell and told me to march out here empty handed."

"Well," Klaw sighed. "You're just in time for the beating."

"Take that hook off, Klaw," Pierce ordered,

110

gesturing with the revolver in his left hand. "I heard what you done to that drover with it last night."

"All right," the one-handed man said as he began to unscrew the steel extremity. "Don't get excited. Your gun might go off by accident and you'll kill one of us too soon."

"Not a chance," Pierce smiled. He eased the hammer down to uncock his Colt. "You ain't getting off the easy way with a bullet."

"Thanks," Klaw replied. Then he hurled the hook into Pierce's face.

The foreman cried out as the hard steel struck his already-damaged cheek, tearing skin and shifting unknitted bone painfully. Klaw lunged forward, his left hand seizing Pierce's gun hand and thrusting it toward the ceiling. His right arm swung, smashing the brass plate at the end of the stump into the point of the foreman's jaw. The blow propelled Neil Pierce's unconscious body into his henchmen.

Joe Felder pulled open the door and entered, three of his fellow ranch hands falling into him. Struggling to keep their balance, the men's hands flailed wildly, one of them tearing Joe's Winchester from his grasp. The rifle clattered to the floor as the cowpunchers prepared to charge the three lawmen.

Tom Becker quickly grabbed the bucket of well water and hurled its contents at the attackers. He swung the wooden container by its handle, shattering the bucket over the skull of one of the aggressors. Klaw's boot lashed out, kicking a heavy-set cowboy on the kneecap. The man staggered, and Klaw moved in to seize the cowboy's axe handle with his left hand as he punched the brass plate into his opponent's mid-section. The blow struck with the force of a rifle butt-stroke. The cowboy doubled up with a groan, and Klaw slammed a knee into his face, knocking the man to the floor in a senseless heap.

Nearly tripping over the man whom Becker had put out of action with the bucket, a wiry young cowhand swung a pick handle at Lazaro Santos. The hunchback's hands flashed and his fists closed around the long hickory shaft. He pulled fiercely, and suddenly the cowpuncher found himself jerked off balance and hurtling into a wall. Another attacker tried to bring a short cudgel down on Lazaro's head, but the hunchback lashed out with the confiscated pick handle. The man screamed in agony as the hard wood crashed into the side of his knee, shattering bone on impact. As the cowhand fell to the floor, Clem Smith swung his club overhead, trying to crack Tom Becker's skull. The former Confederate raised his arms, crossing the wrists to form an *X*. Smith's stick struck the forearms harmlessly as Becker's leg whipped out. His wooden shin swung up between Clem's splayed legs and crashed into his testicles with devastating force. The ranch hand whimpered in agony as he wilted to the floor.

Joe Felder gathered up a fallen club and attacked Klaw, while the man Lazaro had hurled into the wall dashed for the Winchester on the desk. The hunchback met the cowboy's charge and batted the pick handle into his ribs, sending the man tumbling over the length of the desk. The dazed ranch hand began to rise, but Becker brought the bottom of his fist down on the man's neck and knocked him unconscious.

Klaw's forearm blocked Joe Felder's round-

112

house club stroke. He swung the brass plate at the end of his arm, but Joe's open hand deflected the blow. Klaw continued the forward motion of his right arm, bending it and swinging the front of his elbow into Joe's face. The cowboy staggered back, and Klaw hit him with a left jab, followed by a heel kick to the chest. Joe Felder stumbled backward, the blow pitching him through the open office door.

Joe staggered to a halt on the plank walk. Klaw kept moving. He followed the dazed cow puncher and hurled a vicious right cross to Joe's jaw. The brass plate broke three teeth, the force of the blow spinning the ranch hand around. He collapsed, belly-first, on the hitching rail in front of the sheriff's office. Joe tumbled over it gracelessly and fell senseless to the ground.

"That's one hell of a way to start the morning," Becker said, trying to catch his breath.

"It was a hell of a way for them too," Klaw added with a shrug.

Chapter Twelve

ooooooooooooooooooooooooooooooooooo

After locking Pierce and his six henchmen in the jailhouse, Klaw and his deputies assembled the first citizens' militia of Cercano Afeitar. Every man, woman and child congregated in the street to hear the one-handed sheriff address the town.

"You all know why you're here," he began. "We have to form a strong defense to combat Major Nelson's gang tomorrow. That doesn't leave us much time, so we have to do everything in a hurry, and we have to do it right."

Klaw gazed over the faces of the townsfolk. Some—like Robert and Danny Kehoe, Doctor McParlan and Timothy O'Hara—appeared determined. Others—like Arnie, Jerome and Doris Barrow—were almost sick with fear. The people of Cercano Afeitar were a peaceful lot. Fighting and killing were alien to most of them, yet circumstances thrust their town into a violent destiny.

Within twenty-four hours, Cercano Afeitar would become a battlefield.

"Everyone will need a gun," Klaw continued. "If you don't own one, borrow a weapon from one of your neighbors, or come to the sheriff's office. We've got a few spare guns which we recently confiscated. If you don't know which end of a gun does what, tell us now so that we can show you. We want you to kill the enemy, not each other."

"I don't want to kill anyone," Arnie the bartender muttered.

"It's too bad Major Nelson doesn't share your sentiments, feller," Becker growled sourly.

"Besides making sure everybody can hit the broadside of a barn with a rifle, we'll also need a few special items," Klaw told the civilians. "Gather up all the kerosene, gun powder and empty bottles you can find. Bring everything to us."

"And get some roofing nails too," Tom Becker added with a grim smile. "I'm gonna show you folks how to make a bottle grenade, complete with shrapnel."

Klaw continued. "We'll build a barricade at each end of town. Haul out plenty of furniture, barrels, wagons, boxes, anything you can find. We'll also need some good marksmen on the rooftops of the tallest buildings. Lazaro will be in charge of the snipers. You'll pick your shots carefully, keep your heads down until you're ready to use your rifle, and then be damn careful about exposing yourselves. Nelson's boys will be shooting back at you."

"What about the women and children?" Barrow asked fearfully.

"The strongest structure in town is the bank. Women and children will stay there. Sally Clayton?"

"Yes," the pretty blonde replied with surprise.

"I'd like to put you in charge of their safety," Klaw explained. "Do you think you can handle it?"

"Sure," she nodded.

"See here, sheriff," Sherman Kennedy, a portly, balding man complained. "That's my bank you're talking about! By what right do you put some whisp of a girl in command . . ."

"Because Sally can shoot," Klaw told him sharply. "And because you're going to have your able-bodied-male ass out here with the rest of the men."

"Well, I never . . ." the banker huffed.

"Then maybe it's time you tried," Klaw hissed. He mentally reproved himself for being cross with Kennedy. He realized that he had acquired an illogical dislike for bankers after his encounter with Warren Jennings in Great Ford. If Kennedy survived, he'd apologize to him later. "If any of you ladies don't know how to handle a gun, you'd better learn."

"To suggest our womenfolk fight is unchivalrous and insulting, sir," the banker declared.

"They'll only fight if they have to," Klaw replied.

"Shit," Becker groaned. "We'll be lucky if all these sissies don't run out and leave their women behind."

"They won't," Klaw stated. "They have two million and one reasons to stay."

"I understand the two million dollars," Lazaro said. "But what's the other reason?"

116

"Me," the one-handed man replied firmly. "From this moment on, everyone in Cercano Afeitar must realize we're involved in a war. Anyone who flees from this town will be considered a deserter. He or she will then be unceremoniously shot."

Surprised and angry voices rose among the crowd. None were more outraged than the mayor of Cercano Afeitar. "Damn it, Klaw, that's going too far!" Robert Kehoe declared.

"You folks made me sheriff, right? That means I'm supposed to see to the enforcement of the law in this county," Klaw shrugged. "Well, the law that applies in times of war is military justice. It states that desertion is a capital crime. Anyone with a yellow streak had better get out of town right now and forget about his share of the gold. I'll execute any cowardly son of a bitch that leaves this town after today—especially if he deserts brave men under fire. You folks know me well enough to know that I'm not bluffing."

"Well, they may get put to the test mighty quick," Becker commented as he noticed a large group of men on horseback approaching Cercano Afeitar.

Mounted on his handsome Appaloosa, Sam Clayton led the riders. Most of his men held rifles, and all of them wore a sidearm. Klaw gathered up his shotgun and moved through the assembly of Cercano Afeitar citizens. Becker scanned the newly formed militia, noting that only a few of them were armed. Shaking his head with dismay, he limped after the one-handed sheriff. Klaw confronted Clayton at the edge of town.

"I heard they appointed you sheriff, Klaw," the rancher commented as he brought his men to a halt.

"That's a fact," Klaw admitted. "You're bringing quite a group into Cercano Afeitar. Any reason for it?"

Clayton nodded. "My foreman and half a dozen other men rode into town around daybreak. I've come for them."

"They're in the jail," Klaw said. "We arrested them for assault."

"I've heard rumors that a Yankee army major plans to attack Cercano Afeitar," the rancher remarked. "Is there any truth to it?"

"Plenty," the one-handed man confirmed. "Those twenty men with you would sure come in handy against Nelson's gang."

"I never asked this town for anything," Clayton replied coldly. "So I'm not giving it anything now."

"I didn't really think you would," Klaw shrugged.

"Neil Pierce and his men aren't part of Cercano Afeitar."

"They're part of this county," Becker told the rancher as his hand dropped to his holstered Tranter. "And they broke the law here."

"They'll be punished," Clayton stated. "I'll see to that."

"At least here they won't be dangling from the end of a rope," Klaw declared.

"I don't intend to kill my own men," Clayton said angrily. "And I don't intend to leave them helpless in your jail when this major attacks. I don't want my men gunned down in a stinking cell without any chance to defend themselves."

"Our cells don't stink," Becker commented. "I slept in one of them myself."

"You've got a sorry sense of humor for an ex-Confederate officer," the rancher snarled.

"Maybe," Becker allowed, "but your precious bunch of boys planned to put Klaw, Lazaro and me out of action this morning. The bastards were working for Nelson. One of them told us the whole story about an hour ago. You figure they'd still want to work for you if they got their hands on a big enough chunk of gold that would let them live like kings?"

"They're still my men, damn it!"

"Seems to me they're already guilty of desertion in a sense," Becker told Klaw. "Maybe a little public execution will convince these folks we mean business."

"They didn't try to kill us," Lazaro remarked as he and Sally joined Klaw and Becker. Clayton glared at his daughter, but she didn't look away.

"Bullshit," Becker snorted. "Pierce and his boys could have beaten us to death, and I bet they wouldn't have shed any tears if they had!"

"Relax, Tom," Klaw urged. "If we have to fight Clayton's men, we're bound to lose a lot of people. We can't afford that with Major Nelson breathing down our necks. Pierce and his men aren't worth that kind of trouble."

"Then you'll give them to me?" Clayton asked.

"That's right." Klaw nodded.

"I want my daughter to come with me too."

"That's up to her."

"I'm staying here, Father," Sally Clayton declared. "I love Lazaro and I'm not leaving him now."

"The hell you will," the rancher growled as he awkwardly reached for his holstered Colt.

"Don't try it," Klaw warned as he raised the

119

double-barreled Greener.

"You might get me, Klaw," Clayton admitted, "but my men will still blast you and that hunchbacked freak to hell!"

"The buckshot pattern from this shotgun will probably take you and at least two or three of your men out of action," the one-handed man stated, his hook touching the twin triggers. "And Tom is pretty good with that British made sixgun on his hip. I figure he can get about three or four as well."

"Like hell," Becker muttered. "More like five or six."

"The people of Cercano Afeitar need me alive, so they might start shooting as well," Klaw added. "That means a lot of you boys could get blown out of the saddle unless you back off."

"My daughter . . ." Clayton began.

"Your daughter won't love you more if you kill the man she wants to marry," Klaw insisted. "There are some things you can't solve with a gun or a hangman's noose, Clayton. There are some things that don't need to be solved in the first place."

"Sally is gonna marry a fine man," Becker said. "Lazaro is intelligent, hard working and has more guts than ten ordinary men. Why don't you look at *him* instead of the shape of his spine?"

"We'll settle this later," the rancher vowed.

"Fine," Klaw agreed. "Tom, let Pierce and the others go, but tell them that if they show their faces in this town again, until this business with Nelson is over, they're dead."

Becker nodded and limped toward the sheriff's office.

"If my daughter is hurt because she remained in

this town, Klaw," Clayton warned, "you'd better hope Major Nelson kills you before I get the chance!"

Chapter Thirteen

Major Walter Nelson led his men to Cercano Afeitar. His hard features expressed grim determination as he recalled the last two days. His men were not disciplined soldiers, but Nelson had managed to keep them from fighting among themselves or getting drunk the night before the raid. The men under his command were a sorry group of horsemen, and the major had always been a cavalry man. Yet, they were tough and ruthless, and so highly motivated by greed as to make the assault a successful one.

Since Neil Pierce hadn't returned, Nelson assumed that Pierce and his men had either failed to accomplish their mission or never tried. That meant Klaw was still the sheriff of Cercano Afeitar. As if reading his commander's mind, Big Ned urged his horse next to Nelson's mount.

"I sure hope that soldier-boy what fought with

you during the war is ready to meet his Maker," the black man remarked with a wide grin.

"The captain will fight," the major said grimly. "I'd rather he had joined us, or at least left the town."

"He won't be no problem," Ned shrugged.

"Yes he will be," Nelson corrected, "but only a minor one."

"A little trouble is worth two million dollars in gold, eh?" Chad Summer commented as he rode to the other side of Nelson.

"You better enjoy finding your treasure after all these years, white trash," Ned snorted, placing his hand on the long scar Summer's whip had cut into his cheek, " 'cause you ain't gonna live to spend any of it!"

"I'll look forward to settling with you once and for all," Summer growled. "You're gonna wish you'd never left those cotton fields back in Georgia . . ."

"You'll both wait until this mission is over," Nelson ordered. "And personally, I don't care if you kill each other then. Keeping you two from each other's throat has become annoying."

"That so?" Ned inquired. "Well, you won't have to be annoyed with me any more after this job is over, Major."

"That's right," Summer declared. " 'Cause you'll be dead, darkie."

The black man glared at the former Confederate sergeant, but Nelson spoke. "That's enough from both of you," he said. "Ned, you can leave our little group if you so desire, but, until this mission is completed, you're still under my command and you'll do as you're told."

"Yes, sir!" the Negro replied with a mock

salute, almost thumbing his nose at the major. Ned pulled his reins sharply and galloped back to the rear of the riders.

Nelson ignored him. "Mr. Sloane!" he shouted.

"Yes, Major," the second in command answered as he moved his mount forward.

"Prepare to take sixteen men and circle around to the rear of the town."

"A two prong attack," Sloane added, familiar with the technique. "I'll get them into position, sir."

"Good," Nelson replied. "Let's claim the town of Cercano Afeitar."

Tom Becker watched the approaching riders as he jacked a shell into the breech of his Henry carbine. "Here they come," he announced.

Klaw nodded as he thrust Dave Simpson's confiscated .44 Colt into his belt. "Are Lazaro and the snipers in position?"

"Yeah," Becker replied. "And the women and kids are in the bank, except for one or two that insisted on staying with their husbands and helping them reload. Reckon they know the risks involved. My men are at the other end of town. Everybody has ammunition and bottle bombs to spare . . . I hope."

"We'll soon see how well our planning will pay off," the one-handed man remarked. "Good luck, Tom."

Becker held out his hand. "Whatever happens, Klaw," he said. "You're one helluva man."

"You too," Klaw smiled, clasping Becker's hand with his good hand. "Watch yourself, friend."

As the deputy limped away, Klaw ran to the barricade at the edge of town. Robert and Danny Kehoe and Timothy O'Hara waited behind a barricade of chairs, benches, beds, crates, tables and barrels. The one-handed sheriff put a cigar in his mouth and watched Nelson's men draw closer.

"So this is what it feels like to go into combat," Danny commented numbly, his hands tightly closed around the frame of a Winchester rifle.

"This is what waiting feels like," Klaw corrected, striking a match to light his cigar. "The fighting comes next."

"For God's sake, Klaw," Robert Kehoe urged. "Don't go out there."

"I have to," the sheriff replied. "You fellers be ready for the signal."

"Nelson will gun you down for sure!" the mayor insisted.

"Then that'll be the signal," Klaw said as he moved to the edge of the barricade.

Ed Sloane led part of the assault force around the town and the major guided the rest. Nelson considered the barricade a fool's effort to protect Cercano Afeitar. The stacks of furniture and other assorted items were too high for the horses to jump, but it didn't appear to be very sturdy, and Nelson was certain that his men could burn it down if necessary. He failed to notice the wide, damp line stretching across the ground ten feet from the barricade.

"You haven't changed too much, have you, Major?" Klaw stated as he stepped into view.

Nelson jerked the reins sharply, bringing his black mare to a halt. He raised a hand to urge his men to stop. "So, you've come to welcome us in person," the major commented. He saw that Klaw wore his pistol in the button-flap holster on his left

125

hip and another revolver in his belt, but his single hand was empty, and sunlight flashed on the curved steel hook at the end of his right arm.

"I remember how you always planned your battles for afternoon," the one-handed man mused, puffing his stogie gently. "You liked to let the enemy sweat it out all morning before you attacked."

"My tactics are better than yours, Captain," Nelson replied tensely. "You should have joined us when you had the chance."

"Well, Major," Klaw commented, extracting his cigar. "I figure the war ended some time ago. I don't have to take orders from you any more."

"We've got a new war, Klawson," Nelson commented, lowering his hand to his holstered .44 Smith & Wesson. "And we're on opposite sides."

"I know," Klaw agreed, tossing away his cigar butt in a casual manner.

The stogie fell on the damp line between Klaw and the major's raiders. The lit end touched the shallow stream of kerosene. A wall of fire suddenly crackled up from the ground, as if Hell had decided to burst through the earth's crust. Horses bucked and whinnied in terror, and their riders fought to control the frightened animals.

Klaw took advantage of the distraction. Moving to the edge of the barricade, he drew the .44 Colt from his belt and quickly fired a shot at Nelson. Without the major to command the raiders, the other outlaws might be demoralized and retreat. Klaw's bullet struck Nelson in the left biceps, tearing through flesh and muscle, but exiting without hitting bone. The major jerked violently in the saddle and nearly fell from his horse.

The Kehoes and O'Hara poked their rifle barrels

through openings in the barricade. As the kerosene flames began to burn out, the citizens of Cercano Afeitar opened fire on the invaders. Heavy rifle slugs pitched Nelson's men from their saddles; they fell in bleeding, twitching heaps onto the ground. Two bullets hissed past Klaw's head. He raised his .44, squeezed the trigger and shot one of the riders in the center of his chest. The man toppled from the back of his horse as Big Ned swung the muzzle of his Winchester at the retreating figure of Klaw. The one-handed man dodged behind the barricade while the rifle roared, its lead projectile chewing wood from a table stacked on the blockade.

"Did you get Nelson?" Klaw asked Kehoe as he gathered up his shotgun and a canvas sack full of bottle bombs.

"I thought you shot him," the mayor replied, working the lever of his Winchester and aiming through a porthole in the barricade.

"He didn't go down, so I didn't hit him good enough," Klaw admitted.

"But a helluva lot of them are going down," O'Hara declared happily. "We're fighting back, by God!"

Nelson's forces dispersed, but they didn't retreat. The raiders fanned out to encircle the town. Lazaro Santos, positioned on the roof of the hotel, gestured to his fellow snipers located on the saloon roof and the hay loft of the livery stable. The marksmen slowly trained their rifles on the advancing invaders and squeezed off their first shots. Five of Nelson's men fell from their galloping mounts, large caliber bullet holes in their chests. A volley of enemy fire replied to the snipers' attack. One bullet whistled over Lazaro's head as the hunchback hugged the roof. Three rounds tore into the livery stable. Gary Garrison, formerly a clerk in the Cercano Afeitar general store, caught a stray bullet in the stomach. He dropped his Spencer rifle and stumbled over the edge of the hay loft. The young clerk fell to the ground below and died.

Ed Sloane's assault team also met with a barrage of gun fire. Sloane, however, escaped injury, pulled back his men, and ordered them to set fire to the barricade. Ripping the shirts from two of their dead comrades, the raiders set the cloth ablaze. A pair of riders brandished the burning shirts as they galloped to the barricade; Sloane and the others supplied cover fire to keep the defenders pinned down.

"Cute bastards aren't they," Becker muttered as he and his men were forced to leave the bullet riddled barricade. "Well, let's show what smart-asses we can be!"

The deputy and his followers extracted five bottles from a canvas sack. A fuse jutted from the mouth of each bottle, and gun powder and roofing nails comprised the deadly contents of each makeshift grenade. Lighting the fuses, they hurled the bottle bombs over the barricade.

The grenades exploded, two when they hit the ground, and two in mid-air. Number five failed to detonate. One of the raiders was killed instantly, the blast of a bottle bomb tearing man and horse apart. Another was less fortunate. A grenade exploded several feet from the raider, far enough to decrease the full-force of the explosion, but not beyond the range of the shrapnel. Four roofing nails pelleted his chest and face, ripping his flesh and tearing an eye from its socket. Screaming, he fell from the saddle and was stomped to death by his own horse.

Becker watched Sloane's men struggle to control their panic-stricken mounts. He pumped a fresh round into the chamber of his Henry. "Let 'em have it, men," he instructed. Poking the barrel of his carbine through an opening in the barricade, Becker fired. A .44 bullet struck one of the raiders in the back just below the left shoulder blade. The lead projectile punctured the man's heart and burst a gory exit wound in his chest. Other defenders opened fire and more riders fell from their saddles with blood splashed shirts.

"We're winning!" Timothy O'Hara exclaimed as he shot a dismounted raider in the abdomen.

The wounded man fired twice with his Remington revolver. One bullet struck a bed post among the barricade, but the other pierced the opening directly above O'Hara's rifle barrel. The slug struck the restaurant owner in the throat, severed his neck vertebra, and exited at the base of his skull. Timothy O'Hara crumbled to the ground.

"Five men . . . coming in fast to the right," Klaw told Robert and Danny Kehoe, as he touched the lit end of a fresh cigar to the fuse of a bottle grenade.

The mayor and his son followed the sheriff's example and ignited two more bombs. They threw the lethal containers over the blockade. The bottle bombs landed right in the center of the attackers. Exploding almost simultaneously, the grenades hurled tattered, bleeding bodies into the air like discarded rag-dolls. One horse was mangled so badly that one had to look twice in order to tell if it lay on its belly or its back. Another animal had been eviscerated, and three others lay dying from shrapnel wounds.

Only one of the men survived the explosion, He scrambled to his feet, horrified by the decapitated corpse sprawled beside him. His shirt was shredded by flying glass and roofing nails, and his chest felt as if a hundred giant wasps had stung him. Danny Kehoe fired a Winchester round into the wounded man's bloodied chest and terminated his agony.

Only four men in Ed Sloane's detail survived their encounter with Becker's forces at the rear of Cercano Afeitar. Sloane led his trio of men from the battle zone and circled around the town to regroup with Major Nelson's command. Lazaro spied the retreating figures and mistakenly assumed they were trying to attack by entering the poorly barricaded alleys between the various buildings of the town. The hunchback selected a target, aimed and fired. The .44-40 Winchester slug struck one of Sloane's men in the side of the face, tearing his lower jaw bone away and sending the luckless raider cartwheeling awkwardly to the ground.

Sloane and his only two survivors galloped to an area three hundred yards from the town. Major Nelson had dismounted, and Chad Summer was binding his wounded upper-arm with a make-shift bandage. The commander weakly raised his head as Sloane swung down from the saddle.

"So they drove you away too, Mister Sloane," Nelson remarked.

"I'm afraid so, sir," the second in command confessed. "We didn't expect those grenades, and they've got some excellent sharpshooters on their side."

"I know," the major nodded feebly.

"How serious is it, Sergeant?" Sloane asked

Summer.

"Flesh wound," Summer replied. "The bullet went right through the Major's arm, but it didn't do too much damage. But he's gonna have a lot of pain and stiffness for quite a spell with this arm."

"How many men did we lose?" Nelson asked.

"I don't know," Sloane said grimly. "More than half of our troops, I'm sorry to say."

"Jesus," Summer muttered. "What'll we do now?"

"We get reinforcements," Nelson answered.

"Reinforcements?" the ex-Confederate gestured hopelessly. "We don't have any reinforcements! We attacked the goddamn town with everything we had!"

"So next time, we'll use more," the major stated. "We'll get more men. The promise of two million dollars in gold can buy a lot of gunhands. If I have to reduce Cercano Afeitar to a pile of rubble with cannon fire, I'll do it!"

Big Ned and five other men galloped over to the group. "They're tearing us to pieces!" the black man declared.

"I'm well aware of the situation, Ned," Nelson assured him. "We have to retreat."

"Some of your boys managed to get into the town through the alleyways, Major," Ned told him. "What'll we do about them?"

"We leave them," Nelson replied flatly. "We sure as hell can't go in after them." Summer and Sloane helped their commander onto the back of his black mare. "Assemble all the men we can salvage, Mister Sloane, and let's pull out of here."

Two of the invaders who managed to penetrate the town defenses were cut down by rifle fire before they could enter the main street. Seeing the attackers retreat from the frontal assault, Klaw gathered up his shotgun and dashed to the other side of town to investigate.

A lone rider galloped between the hotel and the sheriff's office. Lazaro dropped a bottle grenade into the alley and it exploded behind the invader. The blast sent man and horse hurtling into the main street, their flesh ravaged by shrapnel. Klaw hurried to the fallen raider. The man's right arm hung from a shred of skin as he tried to rise. Drawing his .44 Colt, Klaw shot the outlaw in the temple and put the wounded horse out of its suffering in a similar manner.

Two invaders rode through the alley between the saloon and general store. Doctor McParlan, an excellent rifle marksman and a willing sniper, swung his Springfield down at the pair and squeezed the trigger. The hammer jammed. One of the raiders saw the doctor and fired two revolver rounds into the exposed Irishman. McParlan twitched as the bullets struck his chest and mid-section. Still holding his faulty rifle, the town doctor pitched forward. His body executed a half somersault in mid-air, before it crashed to the ground.

The two raiders emerged from the alley and nearly ran over Klaw. Raising his Greener, the one-handed sheriff pulled the first trigger with his steel hook. A blast of buckshot dissolved the first man's chest in a hideous spray of pink and red stains, the impact of the multiple pellets throwing the corpse to the ground. The other invader died a fraction of a second later as Klaw fired the second barrel. The twelve gauge explosion struck the outlaw under the chin, bursting his skull to pieces.

"That's the last of them, Klaw," Becker declared, limping forward as quickly as his

132

wooden leg would allow. "The rest turned tail and ran like Yankee rabbits!"

Klaw smiled thinly. "You're still a lousy chess player, Nelson," he muttered.

"We did it!" Robert Kehoe exclaimed. "We drove them off!"

"For now," Klaw commented without enthusiasm.

"Klaw," Julie's voice cried. He looked up to see her at a window in the upstairs of the Close Shave Saloon. "Some of them got in on foot! They're still downstairs!"

Chapter Fourteen

∞∞∞∞∞∞∞∞∞∞∞∞∞∞∞∞∞∞∞∞

Lazaro Santos swung over the edge of the hotel roof, dropped to the porch roof and hopped down to the ground as Klaw and Becker approached the saloon. The one-handed man placed the shotgun on the plank walk, opened the button-flap holster and removed his converted Colt .45 revolver.

"Why not use the shotgun?" Tom Becker asked.

"The pattern of buckshot is too indiscriminate," Klaw replied, unscrewing the hook from the end of his arm and replacing it with the Colt. "Julie is still in there, and there might be other civilians inside as well. I don't want one of the bastards to grab an innocent person and be afraid of hitting the wrong target with a blast of buckshot."

"How do you think we should handle this, Klaw?" Lazaro asked as he joined the other two by the saloon.

"First we have to find out where the sons of bitches are," the one-handed sheriff replied. He briefly explained his plan. "All right," he concluded. "Let's get into position and hope everything works."

Klaw and Becker approached the batwings from opposite sides. Carefully, Klaw raised a boot and pushed one of the batwings open. A shot exploded and the bullet smashed into wood, swinging the door back as it chewed a chunk of splinters away. *There's one*, Klaw thought. He turned and nodded to Lazaro.

The hunchback hurled a rock through one of the saloon windows. Another shot shattered more glass and framework. Taking a deep breath, Klaw propelled himself through the batwings, hurtling his body in a low crouch. Most of the furniture had been removed from the saloon to build the barricades. Klaw slid across the sawdust floor, desperately searching for cover as he saw three armed men at the bar.

One of the outlaws trained his revolver on the one-handed man and cocked the hammer. Tom Becker's Tranter roared as he fired from under the batwings. The heavy .45 caliber bullet slammed into the gunman's chest, its impact hurtling him onto the bar. The invader involuntarily pulled the trigger, firing a harmless round into the floor. He slumped to the floor, blood staining his shirt front. His arm tilted over a spittoon, spilling saliva soaked cigar and cigarette butts.

Becker recoiled from the batwings as Klaw rolled rapidly across the saloon floor to the shelter of a ceiling support post. One of the gunmen had already dived over the bar as his comrade, confused by the two threats, selected Becker as the most dangerous opponent. He fired two rounds at the batwings, splintering more wood, but failing to strike flesh. Klaw's marksmanship was better. He slapped the flat of his palm against the hammer of his modified Colt, twice. Two forty-five bullets plowed into the raider's upper chest and throat. The first round pierced the gunman's pectoral muscle, traveled upward and shattered his left collarbone. The other slug struck at an angle, tearing the man's jugular open. He dropped his revolver and seized his severed throat, his eyes bulging as he tried vainly to stop the fountain of blood. He failed. The gunman fell to his knees, slumped on his back and died.

The surviving gunman snapped off a shot at Klaw, then ducked beneath the cover of the bar. A bullet ripped a chunk of wood from the post above Klaw's head, as the one-handed man fired another round, shattering a bottle on a shelf behind the bar.

Lazaro joined Tom Becker at the saloon entrance. The ex-Confederate blasted two bullets into the bar and the hunchback burst two more bottles with Winchester fire. Klaw rose to his knees and thrust a thumb to his chest, then pointed at the bar. Becker nodded in agreement.

"Let's give the sheriff what he wants," the deputy told Lazaro. "Keep that bastard pinned down until Klaw can make his move."

Becker's Tranter and Lazaro's rifle bombarded the bar and its surrounding shelves with bullets. The mirror behind the counter exploded, showering the terrified invader with shards of glass. Klaw half-ran, half-crawled to the bar. Becker and Lazaro ceased fire. The one-handed man squatted low at the counter and waited.

The gunman slowly ventured a peek over the top of the bar—Lazaro and Becker still lurked at the batwings, but he couldn't see Klaw. Stretching his arm across the counter, he cocked the hammer of his Whitney Navy revolver and aimed at the two deputies by the swinging doors.

Klaw's hand snaked out, his strong fingers closing on his opponent's wrist. Twisting hard, Klaw wrenched the gun from the outlaw's grasp. The Whitney fell to the floor, striking the hammer and firing a .36 caliber lead ball into the ceiling. Klaw pulled the man's captive arm to the left, then rose to backhand the barrel of his Colt across the invader's face.

Becker and Lazaro entered the saloon as Klaw hauled the stunned outlaw across the bar. The man fell to the floor heavily. His jaw began to swell and blood trickled from the corner of his mouth. Klaw seized the raider by his shirt front and jammed the muzzle of his Colt under the outlaw's chin.

"Now, you can either answer some questions, or I'll blow your head off," Klaw told his captive. "How many of you managed to get inside this saloon?"

"Go to hell," the gunman muttered thickly.

"Have it your way, feller," the one-handed man rasped. "Let's see if I can't get you to be a little more cooperative. Maybe if I take one of those broken whiskey bottles behind the bar and shove the jagged end into your face, you'll feel more sociable."

"I'll see what we have to choose from," Becker stated as he limped around the bar. "Would you rather cut him with a red-eye bottle or just old rotgut?"

137

"No," the prisoner urged. "There were four of us . . . Me, Pete, Jake and Jimmy!"

"Two are lying dead on the floor and you're number three," Klaw remarked. "What happened to the fourth one?"

"Don't lie to us," Becker added.

The gunman trembled fearfully. "Jimmy's upstairs," he replied.

"He'd better be," Klaw said grimly. "Watch him," the sheriff told his deputies as he moved to the stairwell.

Jimmy Eaton wished he'd never heard of Major Walter Nelson or the town of Cercano Afeitar. The raid was supposed to be easy. Nelson had said that Cercano Afeitar was populated with weaklings and cowards; claiming the two million dollars in Confederate gold would be a cinch, so he said! *Shit*, Eaton thought. *I'll be lucky to get out of here alive!*

He leaned over the upstairs railing and noticed a long, distorted shadow on the wall below. Wood creaked. A man appeared on the stairs, a gun in his hand. Eaton didn't waste time trying to identify the figure below. Aiming his .44 Remington revolver, Eaton cocked the hammer and fired.

Klaw saw the gunman in the upstairs hallway a second before Eaton squeezed the trigger. The one-handed man jumped back as the bullet smashed into the wooden step where his foot had been a moment earlier. Klaw's hand fanned the Colt's hammer and raised the revolver. A .45 slug splintered the upstairs railing. Eaton recoiled with alarm as Klaw dashed up the stairs.

The gunman fired another round at the approaching lawman, his bullet striking a

138

handrail, chipping wood harmlessly. Klaw threw himself to the landing as Eaton snapped off a third shot. The .44 projectile burrowed into the wall behind Klaw. Fragments of plaster tumbled down on the one-handed man's head. Klaw hit the hammer of his Colt again. A .45 bullet struck a wooden door frame behind Eaton, but it was close enough to frighten the gunman into retreating.

Klaw raced to the head of the stairs as his opponent fired a fourth shot. The slug ripped out a chunk from the bannister post near the one-handed man. Jimmy Eaton shuffled backward down the hallway, trying to aim his smoking Remington at Klaw. He failed to hear the door open behind him.

Julie stepped from her room and thrust an H&R .32 caliber revolver into Eaton's back. "Hold it right there, mister," she ordered. "Drop the gun."

Eaton's body tensed and he raised his arms woodenly, the Remington still in his fist. Klaw rose from the cover of the bannister post and approached the outlaw, his thumb on the hammer of his converted Colt. Eaton's eyes darted rapidly in their sockets. He was a trapped and desperate animal—and that made him more dangerous than ever.

"I told you to drop that gun," Julie repeated, shoving the muzzle of her H&R harder into his back.

"Whatever you say, lady," Eaton replied as he began to lower his arms.

"Move away from him, Julie!" Klaw yelled.

Jimmy Eaton suddenly pivoted sharply. An elbow struck Julie's gunhand, knocking the revolver from her grasp. Klaw raised the Colt attached to his right arm, but Eaton and the girl were too close for the sheriff to claim a clear target. Swiftly, Eaton moved behind Julie, snaking his free arm around her throat and pressing the muzzle of his Remington against her temple.

"Drop your gun or I'll kill her," Eaton told Klaw.

"I can't drop it," the one-handed man answered, holding out his right arm for Eaton's inspection.

"Jesus," the outlaw whispered, wondering what kind of man has a revolver growing at the end of his arm. He automatically stepped backward, dragging his captive with him. Julie tried to break free, but Eaton tightened his strangle hold. She gasped as the forearm at her throat cut off her breath.

"If you hurt her," Klaw said flatly, "you're dead."

Eaton cocked the hammer of his Remington. "She's gonna be my ticket out of here."

"You're not leaving this saloon or this town with her," Klaw told him. "She'll be your ticket for Boot Hill unless you let her go right now and drop your gun."

"I'll drop it," Eaton agreed.

He quickly swung the barrel from Julie's head towards Klaw. The modified Colt boomed as Klaw snap-aimed, putting all his years of pistol marksmanship into the shot. A fat .45 bullet burned air scant inches from Julie's right ear and struck Jimmy Eaton in the face. The heavy lead slug smashed through the outlaw's clenched teeth, the impact hurling Eaton backward. He squeezed the trigger of his Remington as he released Julie, his arms flapping wildly, attempting to regain his balance. The outlaw's bullet tore harmlessly into the ceiling. Jimmy Eaton backed into a window at the end of the hall, his torn face a mask of pain. The glass and framework refused to support Eaton's weight. He crashed through the window and screamed as he plunged to the ground two stories below.

"Are you all right?" Klaw asked Julie as she rushed into his arms.

"Yes," she whispered, burying her face in his shoulder. "Oh, God! Was I frightened!"

"Me too," Klaw admitted. "But why weren't you over at the bank with the rest of the ladies?"

"I thought I could help more if I stayed here," she shrugged. "Guess I figured wrong."

"You did fine," Klaw assured her, kissing the girl's cheek. "We're both still alive, aren't we?"

Klaw rejoined Tom Becker and Lazaro Santos downstairs. Becker helped himself to a bottle of whiskey that somehow had survived the previous gunfight. The hunchback smiled at Klaw.

"Where's our prisoner?" the one-handed man asked.

"I tied him to the hitching rail out front," Becker replied, swigging a long swallow from the bottle. He grimaced at the raw taste of the cheap whiskey. "We were about to run upstairs and give you a hand—no pun intended—when that feller came flying down into the street. He damn near landed on Kennedy. I thought that fat little banker was gonna have a heart attack for a minute."

"What matters is that it's finally over," Lazaro stated.

"Hardly," Klaw told them. "Major Nelson will be back."

"Crap," Becker muttered. "After the way we

beat him off? We killed at least half his men today, for crissake.''

"So, he'll get more men, and he'll be more careful the next time,'' the one-handed man declared. "And there will be a next time. How much trouble do you think he'll have getting men to follow him for a chunk of two million dollars in gold?''

"None at all, if he goes to the right places,'' Becker admitted. "And a couple of those places are around these parts too. Maybe we can dig up the gold and take off before he can form a new gang and return to Cercano Afeitar.''

"And maybe it'll take us weeks to find the gold,'' Klaw replied. "Besides, as long as Nelson's alive, he'll try to hunt us down.''

"Yeah,'' Becker agreed. "And a hunchback, a feller with one hand and another with a wooden leg wouldn't be hard to locate. None of us exactly blend with the crowd.''

"What can we do?'' Lazaro asked. "Do we wait for Nelson to return?''

"No,'' Klaw said. "We'll go after him first.''

Chapter Fifteen

Klaw had some difficulty convincing the citizens of Cercano Afeitar that it was necessary to hunt down Major Nelson and the remnants of his gang. Three townsfolk had been killed defending Cercano Afeitar, and the numerous corpses that littered the street—especially those mutilated by grenade or shotgun blasts—were grizzly examples of what ugly forms sudden death can assume. However, when Klaw explained that Major Nelson would return more determined than ever to destroy the town, several men volunteered to join the posse.

Although Robert Kehoe wanted to ride with Klaw, the sheriff insisted that he remain to organize the town's defense, in case Nelson's men somehow evaded the posse and attacked the town before the others could return. The mayor's son, Danny Kehoe, joined the lawmen, along with

Arnie the bartender who overcame his previous fear and volunteered. Albert Lane's fifteen-year-old son, Alan, decided to join them, and Doctor McParlan's nephew, Sean, a sixteen-year-old apprentice under the slain doctor, shared his uncle's fighting spirit and stubborn courage.

Most of the townsmen were too old or too frightened to join the man hunt. The posse numbered eleven men when they finally mounted their horses and rode from Cercano Afeitar in search of Walter Nelson and his men.

"We'll be lucky if the major's people don't chop us to bits this time," Tom Becker complained, as he rode his Morgan stallion beside Klaw's mount.

"Nelson told me he had forty men," the one-handed man replied. "He lost twenty-six today. That means he only has fourteen left."

"Unless he's already gotten reinforcements," Becker commented sourly. "Besides, fourteen is still more than we've got."

"Our people have bottle grenades that should give us an extra edge," Klaw stated. "Nelson is wounded, and some of his men were probably hurt as well. Let's hope they've returned to their old bivouac area to lick their wounds and aren't expecting us."

"Our jailbird gave us a good description of their camp and its location," Lazaro Santos remarked. "We'll soon know if the major is still there or not."

"Well, so far, Nelson's boys haven't been trying to conceal their tracks," Becker mused, studying the hoofprints on the dirt road. "If they don't start covering up their trail, we shouldn't have any trouble finding them—providing the sun doesn't set first," Becker added, considering the position

144

of the hot orange ball uncomfortably close to the horizon. "We can't do any tracking at night. Torches or kerosene lanterns would be seen by the enemy miles away."

"Then we'd better find the camp soon," Klaw commented gently.

The hoofprints continued on the road for two miles and then branched off across the prairie. The trail led them to a forest just as twilight descended.

"Nelson's camp should be in that patch of woods," Becker remarked. "But it's hard to say if they've posted look-outs or not. Hell, those trees could be full of men. There's lots of cover for them up there, and damn little for us if we go galloping across the prairie like a bunch of young bulls."

"We'll dismount," Klaw said, as he swung down from his saddle. "The horses will get in the way among the trees and bushes."

"If you get your share of the gold, you'll be able to get that saber fixed," Becker commented, noticing the threaded bolt jutting from a sword scabbard on Klaw's saddle. "It needs a new handle."

"No, it doesn't," Klaw told him. "I had a blacksmith in Colorado alter the saber for me."

Before Becker could ask why the handle had been removed, Lazaro spoke. "If we approach the forest on foot, sentries or snipers will see us."

"I'm going ahead to investigate the area," Klaw replied. "The rest of you will wait here."

"Like hell I will," Becker growled. "There are probably guards posted around Nelson's camp. I can handle a knife better than any man here, and you might need my help up there."

"That's true, Tom," Klaw agreed. "But it's also true that you can't move around silently with that wooden leg.''

"I'll go with you," the hunchback volunteered.

"Sorry, Lazaro," the one-handed man said. "You haven't been trained in this sort of thing, and I can't teach you how to sneak into an enemy encampment now."

"All right, Klaw," Becker sighed. "Do you want to take along some bottle grenades?"

"Yeah," Klaw answered. "And I'll need a horseblanket too."

He sat down on a rock and pulled off his boots. Although the others were puzzled by his actions, Becker understood. "You want me to cut up the blanket for you?" he asked, removing his saddle from the back of the Morgan.

"I'd appreciate it," Klaw replied. "I could also use some help binding my feet with the cloth. It's pretty hard to tie knots with only one hand."

"What are you doing?" Danny Kehoe asked, as he watched Becker slice through a horseblanket with his Arkansas Toothpick.

"Do-it-yourself moccasins," Klaw explained. "The Indians make them a lot better, but they'll serve as temporary footgear."

"Lazaro," Becker said. "How about putting these things on Klaw's feet? Kneeling or stooping with this damn leg is a pain in the ass."

The hunchback bound the one-handed man's feet with the coarse wool cloth. Klaw nodded with approval as he rose. The "moccasins" would allow him to walk almost noiselessly, and his feet would be protected. Becker handed him a sack containing four bottle grenades.

"If I find the camp, I'll signal you to advance by striking a match," Klaw told the others. "If I don't come back, Tom is in charge. He'll decide

146

whether you continue after Nelson or turn back."

Klaw left the Greener shotgun with his men and moved to the treeline. He didn't attempt to conceal himself as he walked to the edge of the forest. If anyone was watching, they would already know that the posse was there and that Klaw was coming. With every step, he was prepared to dive to the ground if he saw movement among the trees or a flash of metal. Klaw reached the treeline without incident.

He moved surreptitiously among the bushes and trees, his single hand ready to drop the sack and draw his Remington derringer. The increasing darkness worried him. Perhaps the major had changed the location of his camp, or their prisoner may have lied about the site of Nelson's headquarters. If they didn't find it by nightfall, they'd have to abandon the search, but then he saw a flickering yellow light in the distance.

Taking more care than ever to avoid making noise, Klaw approached the encampment. The tall, wide shapes of tents lurked among the shadows surrounding the campfire. Several men squatted by the fire, eating beans from tin plates and drinking hot coffee. Horses were housed within a rope corral. Scanning the bivouac area, he located a single sentry. The man's expression revealed weary boredom, but he still appeared to be alert, and he held his Winchester as if he was ready to use it at a moment's notice. Cautiously, the one-handed man withdrew and returned to the edge of the forest.

Striking a match, he signaled his posse to come forward. When the group assembled, Klaw explained where the bivouac area was. He broke the posse into details, assigning three men to follow Becker, three to join Lazaro, and the remaining two for himself. He quickly explained how they should position themselves around the camp, warning them not to open fire until he tossed the first bottle grenade into the enemy's lair.

When the campfire came into view, the teams divided. Becker's detail moved to the right, Lazaro's to the left, and Klaw led Danny Kehoe and Sean McParlan forward. Drawing closer to the camp, Klaw's team stopped by the cover of a large bush and extracted bottles from their sacks, preparing for the assault.

Danny Kehoe's hand urgently tapped Klaw's shoulder. The one-handed man turned. The sentry had changed position and now walked toward the bush, his Winchester held ready at his hip.

Klaw didn't waste time wondering what had drawn the man's attention. Perhaps he'd caught a glimpse of clothing among the leaves of the bush, or moonlight may have reflected on a glass bottle or Klaw's hook. The guard had to be dealt with quickly. Klaw picked up a stone and placed it into Sean McParlan's hand. He pointed to another bush several feet to the rear. McParlan nodded in agreement. Klaw moved to the edge of the shrubbery and gestured to Sean. The youth threw the stone, striking the other bush with a loud rustle of leaves. The sentry swung his rifle towards the sound and Klaw moved forward.

Stepping on his padded feet, he crept up behind the distracted guard. His left hand shoved the Remington derringer into the small of the man's back. The sentry stiffened as the hard metal pressed into his spine.

"No tricks," Klaw whispered harshly. "Put the gun down slowly. If you try something, I'll break your back and leave you paralyzed for life."

The guard obeyed the order without protest. He carefully stooped and placed the Winchester on the grass. Klaw's right arm swung, the curve of his steel hook clubbing the sentry behind the ear. With a soft moan, the man fell forward. Klaw caught the unconscious guard and dragged him behind the bush. Danny and Sean relieved the sentry of his sidearm and used his own belt to bind his hands behind his back.

"Do you think they're in position yet," Danny asked softly, gagging their captive with a neckerchief.

"I sure hope so," Klaw replied, striking a match. "Let's start the show."

Lighting a bottle bomb, the one-handed man hurled it into the camp. The grenade landed by the largest tent. Canvas and poles collapsed, and bleeding, screaming men dragged themselves from the fallen tent. The explosion signaled the rest of the posse, their rifles firing all around the bivouac area. Bullets crashed into startled figures. One outlaw dropped his plate of beans and dragged a revolver from its hip holster as two slugs struck him in the chest and hurled him backward. The man fell into the campfire.

More bottle grenades flew into the camp. The bombs leveled the remaining tents and hurled mangled corpses into the air. Bullets continued to cut down the outlaws in a vicious crossfire. There was no shelter from the deadly volleys of lead. Few managed to fire a single shot before lethal projectiles snuffed the life from their bloodied bodies.

"Hold your fire!" Klaw shouted.

The silence that followed seemed more ominous than the previous barrage of gunshots and explosions. However, a handful of men in the camp had escaped the posse's ruthless attack. The survivors stood slowly, their empty hands raised above their heads.

"Don't shoot," Chad Summer begged, as he painfully rose, blood oozing from a bullet-smashed kneecap. "We've had enough! We surrender!"

"Everybody stay where you are," Klaw instructed. "Keep me covered and watch for wounded men that might be playing possum."

Klaw stepped forward and entered the camp. The stench of burning human flesh mingled with the odor of cordite. Summer and three men were all that remained of the gang. Klaw scanned the corpses as he drew closer. He frowned when he failed to find the major's body.

"Where's Nelson?" he asked.

"He . . . he rode out of here with Sloane and Big Ned," Summer replied through clenched teeth, as he put too much weight on his injured leg. "He put me in charge 'cause he didn't want me and the nigger together. We hate each other's guts, and the major knows I'd kill that darkie if I got the chance."

"Where did he go?"

"Rio Verde," Summer said. "It's a town about eight or ten miles west. Nelson plans to hire some more men there."

"I know about Rio Verde, Klaw," Becker announced. "This jasper's probably tellin' the truth. Rio Verde is populated with lots of down and out saddle bums, Missouri outlaws and army deserters."

"Sounds like an ideal recruiting station," Klaw commented grimly.

"You got it," Tom Becker confirmed. "If

Nelson can't find himself a bunch of hard cases and cutthroats in Rio Verde, he can't find them anywhere."

"Well, he's already managed it once," the one-handed man observed. "So we'd better stop him before he does it again."

"I know the way to Rio Verde," Becker stated with a chuckle. "I sort of passed through there once."

Klaw smiled. He'd almost forgotten that Becker was a former outlaw himself. "All right," he agreed. "Night is settling in. That means we'll have to travel by lantern light. The trip to Rio Verde will be highly dangerous for anyone that rides with Tom and me. We'll be mighty clear targets if Nelson decides to break camp somewhere between here and Rio Verde."

"I'll go with you," Lazaro announced. "I've been involved in this from the beginning, and I want to be with you for the finish."

"Just hope Nelson hasn't already got himself a new gang," Becker stated grimly. "Or it might be *us* that get finished!"

Chapter Sixteen

Klaw, Tom Becker and Lazaro Santos rode on to Rio Verde, while the rest of the posse escorted the surviving members of the outlaw gang back to Cercano Afeitar. The posse resembled a cluster of enormous fire-flies, as they galloped away with their lanterns burning.

Since Becker was familiar with the town of Rio Verde and his tracking skill was superior to his companions', he took the lead. They rode more than three hours before they discovered remnants of a campfire. Dismounting, Becker knelt by the ashes, touching the charred wood gingerly.

"It's pretty warm," he commented. "I'd say the major was here about two hours ago."

"Why would they stop here?" Lazaro asked.

"Maybe they had to," Klaw replied, as he noticed a strip of half-burned cloth among the ashes. Pulling it free, he found that it was part of a shirt, carefully cut, and stained with blood.

"What is it?" the hunchback wanted to know.

"A bandage," Klaw said. "Apparently, Major Nelson's wounded arm needed a fresh dressing."

"I hope that means they're really dragging ass," Becker remarked. "Otherwise, Nelson might have a small army waiting for us at Rio Verde."

"And I hope they do not stop to set up camp again," Lazaro stated. "Carrying these lanterns on horseback is like wearing a sign that says *shoot me.*"

"If we didn't use the lanterns we'd be taking a greater risk," Klaw told him. "We could ride smack into low hanging tree limbs, or one of our horses could break a leg in a prairie dog hole."

"Yeah," Becker agreed. "And even with the lanterns we can't ride at a gallop. At least Nelson will have to move just as slowly."

"But he has a head start," Klaw reminded them. "So we'd better keep moving."

They entered Rio Verde after midnight. The town had been named in honor of a narrow greenish-blue river that had dried up before any of the current inhabitants were born. Although Rio Verde was designed in the same manner as Cercano Afeitar, the businesses differed greatly. Rio Verde had no bank, barber shop or hotel, but it featured a livery stable with a corral, a general store, a gunsmith, a doctor's office, two saloons and a tiny sheriff's office.

"Rio Verde doesn't have a real jail," Becker explained as they rode into town. "Sheriff Pat Derrick used to be an owl-hoot himself, and he knows what sort of people the place attracts. You can get away with a lot in Rio Verde, but if the law takes notice of you, you're in big trouble. Derrick will either run you out of town or kill you, whatever pleases him. He doesn't believe in trials. He just shoots fellers instead. Derrick knows most of the fellers in town are sensitive about seeing hangings, so he never strings anybody up.''

"Sounds like a compassionate, civic-minded feller," Klaw muttered.

"Yeah." Becker chuckled. "And he doesn't like other lawmen poking around in his town. That's why I advised you to take your badges off before we got here. Most of the fellers in Rio Verde would be apt to put a bullet in you, if they saw a tin star on your chest, and Pat Derrick wouldn't do a damn thing about it.''

"Do you think he'll help us?" Lazaro asked.

"I doubt it," Becker replied. "I just hope he agrees to stay out of our way.''

They rode to the sheriff's office and dismounted, drawing their long arms from saddle boots. Klaw rapped on the door with his steel hook to avoid startling a trigger-happy lawman before opening it. A young, pale-faced man, with a weak chin, a needle-nose, and wide watery eyes, sat behind a battered old desk with three bullet holes in its frame. He stared up at the trio, looking with consternation at Klaw's shotgun and the deputies' rifles.

"Where's Sheriff Derrick?" Becker demanded.

"He ain't here," the young man replied. "Some feller burst in here the other day and tried to kill him. He put a bullet in the sheriff before old Pat could gun him down.''

"But Derrick's still alive," Becker clucked his tongue. "Figures that bastard would be too mean to die.''

"He's in the hospital," the kid said. "I'm
154

Deputy Mullet. Can I help you fellers?"

"Sure hope so," Klaw nodded, extracting his badge from a pocket. "We're lawmen from the town of Cercano Afeitar."

"I know the place," Mullet stated. "Seems to me their sheriff is a fat old guy named Winn."

"A feller murdered Winn a couple days ago," the one-handed man replied. "The same feller we're looking for."

"Holy Hanna," the young deputy whispered with awe. "And you figure this owl hoot is here in Rio Verde?"

"Save the act, kid," Becker snorted. "We know what sort of town this is. You've got more wanted men in Rio Verde than a buffalo has tics, so just tell us if you've seen the men we're looking for."

"Men?" Mullet raised an eyebrow. "I thought you were looking for only one man."

"There's three of them traveling together," Klaw explained. "Walter Nelson has a wounded arm or shoulder. He might be wearing a cavalry major's uniform, but he probably removed the hat and tunic since you've got a lot of army deserters here. A big black feller called Ned and another man named Sloane are with him."

"Sloane is about my size," Mullet announced, "but he has black hair and a little mustache!"

"Then they are here," Lazaro asked urgently.

"Sure are," the deputy nodded. "I seen 'em ride into town a couple hours ago."

"Can you show us where they are?" Klaw inquired.

"Better than that," Mullet replied. "I'll take you there myself."

The deputy rose and walked to the door, adjusting the gunbelt around his narrow waist.

"Goddamn fugitives think they can do anything they please in our town," he huffed, trying to sound authoritative, but his shaking hands betrayed his fear. Mullet reminded Klaw of a younger, thinner version of the late Sheriff Winn. "We'll teach 'em. We'll make an example of 'em for the rest of the scum in this town."

"Sure, kid," Becker muttered as he followed Mullet to the door.

The young lawman led Klaw and his men directly across the street to the livery stable. "They're inside," Mullet explained. "The owner's letting them stay there tonight. The feller with the shot up arm claimed some highwaymen jumped them on the road and . . ."

"And you're leading us right up to the front door, as if we were going to church on Sunday morning," Klaw growled, moving quickly to the side of the building. "Why the hell didn't you tell us they were right across the street?"

"Hell, they're asleep," Mullet assured them. "You don't have to worry none."

"Look, boy," Becker hissed, putting his back against the wall of the livery stable. "These men aren't a bunch of saddle bums. They're so mean we'll probably have to kill them twice."

"Maybe I'd better go tell Sheriff Derrick," the deputy suggested in a quivering voice.

Klaw, Lazaro and Becker ignored him as they crept closer to the entrance of the livery stable. The sound of a hammer cocking back startled them. Turning, they saw Mullet aiming his revolver at them.

"Drop them irons," he demanded.

"I'll be a son of a bitch," Becker moaned.

"We'll talk about your ambitions later," Klaw

156

rasped.

"So Nelson bought himself a lawman," Becker growled, putting down his Henry carbine. "I should have guessed, damn it. Wearing this tin star has made me careless."

"Keep your hands away from your short guns," Mullet warned. "And get inside."

They entered the livery stable. A kerosene lantern suspended from the ceiling provided dim yellow illumination within the building. Major Walter Nelson nodded a grim greeting as Klaw, Becker and Lazaro filed inside. Nelson had removed his jacket and cavalry hat, but he still wore his gunbelt and saber. His left arm rested in a sling tied to the back of his neck.

"I'm glad you could join us, Captain," he stated in a flat, emotionless voice. "Ned! Mister Sloane!"

The big Negro and Nelson's second in command emerged from a stall. Ned glared at them as he stepped forward with his Winchester braced against his hip. Ed Sloane's features remained impassive as he cocked the hammer of his Colt and advanced.

"Get their sidearms," Nelson ordered.

"Sure enough," Ned smiled widely.

The major's men carefully approached their captives from behind. Ned removed Becker's Tranter, and Sloane opened Klaw's flap holster. He examined the modified Colt revolver with curiosity. "Don't forget about the captain's derringer," Nelson told his men. "And I understand this Johnny-Reb is supposed to be quite good with that knife of his."

"I'd like this Southern white trash try to use that knife on me right now," Ned snickered, drawing

157

the Arkansas Toothpick from its sheath.

"Their other guns are right outside," Mullet said.

"Well, we don't want to attract attention, you idiot," Nelson snapped. "Bring them in here, for God's sake!"

Sloane piled the confiscated weapons on a bale of hay, and the deputy hurried outside to fetch the rifles and shotgun. Nelson shook his head with regret. "You were a fool, Captain," he sighed. "You should have known better than to side with those dolts back in Cercano Afeitar."

"But I won't have any trouble living with myself, Major," the one-handed man replied.

"No, you won't," Nelson agreed. "Because you won't be alive much longer."

"Major, I've done as you told me . . ." Mullet began as he returned with the guns in his arms.

"And you'll be paid," Nelson said. "Now, shut up."

"You won't get away with this, Major," Klaw told him. "The rest of my posse is on its way here."

"I don't believe you," Nelson declared.

"It doesn't matter if you do or not," the one-handed man shrugged. "We found your camp and your men talked. That's how we tracked you here."

"Rio Verde has a certain reputation," the major said. "You made a lucky guess."

"That's bullshit and you know it," the one-handed man commented. "My men will be here any minute."

"Why didn't they come with you?" Nelson demanded.

"A large group of riders would attract too much

158

attention," Klaw lied smoothly. "We rode in to scout the area first—to find where you were hidden."

"Even if it's true," the major declared, nervously pacing the stable, "we'll be ready for them."

"Hold on, Major," Mullet said, as he dumped the rifles and shotgun on the weapons pile. "You said there would be no trouble here in Rio Verde!"

"This town thrives on trouble," Nelson scoffed.

"Sheriff Derrick is over in the hospital, and his brothers are with him," the deputy explained. "They're almost as mean as he is. If there's any shooting, they'll be over here like a bunch of bobcats!"

"Stop whimpering, white boy," Ned snarled. "We can kill these crippled-up freaks without shooting them, so don't wet your pants."

"And just how do you think you can kill a white man without using a gun," Klaw asked haughtily. "How about it, nigger?" Klaw figured that if he provoked Ned, the black man might become angry, and an angry man is careless.

Ned's eyes bulged with fury. He swung the butt of his Winchester at Klaw's head. The one-handed man's left forearm blocked the rifle stock as he drove the curve of his steel hook into Ned's midsection. With a gasp, the big black man doubled up, and Klaw's left fist smashed into the side of his jaw.

Big Ned stumbled backward. Klaw's foot lashed out, kicking the frame of the Winchester and ripping it from the black man's grasp. The steel hook flashed, the sharp point tearing the black man's shirt. Ned cried out as a trail of blood trickled from his chest. Klaw's fist delivered a fast hard jab to his opponent's jaw, and Big Ned fell heavily to the floor.

His hands darting to the chain around his waist, Ned suddenly pulled the iron belt free and lashed out at Klaw's legs. The metal links snaked around the one-handed man's ankles. Ned tugged sharply and Klaw's feet jerked out from under him. He crashed to the floor as Big Ned scrambled upright.

"That's enough," Nelson ordered.

The black man ignored him as he swung the chain overhead. Klaw rolled over. The heavy iron links slammed across his back like an iron whip. The one-handed man groaned, and Ned swung his weapon again.

"Stop them, Mister Sloane," Nelson commanded.

"Yes, sir," the dapper gunman nodded.

Sloane stepped towards Ned and Klaw. Suddenly, Lazaro seized him, twisting the Colt from Sloane's hand. Becker also took advantage of the distraction Klaw had provided. He drew his .32 caliber S&W hide-out revolver. Becker's diminutive pistol barked twice, one bullet breaking Mullet's collarbone and the other tearing his deltoid muscle apart. His arm rendered totally useless, the deputy dropped his revolver, staggered back two feet and passed out.

The powerful Lazaro soon overpowered Sloane. He raised Nelson's second in command off the floor and dropped to one knee, bringing Sloane down hard. A loud crack seemed to fill the livery stable as Ed Sloane's back connected with Lazaro's knee. He gasped as he realized his spine had been broken in two. The hunchback allowed the dying man to fall to the floor.

Ned's chain whirled and Klaw rolled out of its path. Metal struck wood. Klaw's opponent swung again, Klaw turning his head and shoulders quickly as the iron links smashed into the floor. Bracing himself with his shoulders and upper-back, Klaw lashed out with his foot. The bottom of his boot connected with Ned's face. The black man staggered, blood pouring from his broken nose and split lower lip.

Klaw rose swiftly as the stunned Negro slashed out with his chain. The one-handed man dodged, and then suddenly charged Big Ned. Steel flashed under Ned's chin as Klaw's right arm executed a fast backhand stroke. The powerful black hulk seemed to crumble to the floor, his hands releasing the chain to seek his damaged throat. Blood gushed from the ghastly wound, pouring through Ned's fingers, staining the floor of the livery stable. Big Ned's body twitched briefly, as Klaw shook flecks of blood from the tip of his hook.

Major Nelson didn't see his men die—he was too busy. When the prisoners seized their opportunity to turn the figurative table on their captors, the major rushed to the cover of a stack of nail kegs. Becker saw the fleeing figure and fired two fast rounds at him. One small .32 bullet plowed harmlessly into a keg, the other—by sheer freak accident—smashed into the holster on Nelson's hip. Nelson poked the barrel of his .44 Smith and Wesson around the edge of a keg. He tried to cock the hammer, but it refused to move. Becker's stray bullet had smashed the revolver's cylinder. Nelson furiously hurled the useless gun aside and ran through a side door leading into the corral.

Lazaro dashed to the door and discovered Nelson had bolted it from the outside. "*Cristo,*" the hunchback groaned. "If he gets a horse, he may escape!"

"No, he won't," Becker vowed as he gathered up his Henry carbine and tossed Lazaro the Winchester. "We'll get the bastard." He turned to pitch the shotgun to the one-handed man.

Klaw wasn't there.

When he saw Nelson flee outside, Klaw guessed the major's escape plan. He ran from the livery stable to the sheriff's office, twisting the steel hook from the end of his arm. Klaw hung the hook on his belt as he reached his horse tied to the hitching rail. Quickly, he drew his saber from its scabbard on the saddle.

Major Nelson climbed onto the bare back of his black mare in the corral. Scraping its sides with his spurs, he urged the animal into a sudden gallop. The horse approached the fence and executed a desperate jump. It sailed over the barrier, nearly tripping on the top rail. Nelson spurred his mount savagely, driving the mare down the center of the street.

Then he saw Klaw, standing in his path, a modified cavalry saber attached to the end of his right arm.

"Very well, Captain," he snarled through clenched teeth, as he drew his own sword. "If you wish to die by cold steel, I'm happy to oblige you!"

He charged Klaw, slashing his saber at the man on foot. Klaw raised the long blade at the end of his arm, steel blocking steel. Nelson jerked the mane of his horse, forcing the animal to the right, as he swung his sword again. Klaw side-stepped the descending blade and caught his opponent's arm. With a sharp pull, he hauled Nelson off the back of his mare to the ground.

The major slashed at Klaw's legs, but the one-handed man jumped out of the blade's path. Nelson rose, smiling, and assumed a fencer's position. Becker and Lazaro emerged from the livery stable to watch the combatants square off. The major lunged forward, his sword neatly slipping under Klaw's blade, the tip raking the one-handed man's ribs. Klaw countered with a fast series of slashing strokes. Nelson laughed as he easily parried each move.

"Damn it," Becker muttered as he raised his Henry to his shoulder. "If they didn't change positions so fast, I could pick that son of a bitch off."

The long blades clashed again, Nelson driving Klaw back with rapid well placed strokes. The one-handed man blocked each attack, but Nelson twisted his saber adroitly and sliced a long, bloody furrow in Klaw's forearm.

"You're out-classed, Captain," the major declared. "Drop your guard, and I promise to make it as quick as possible."

"All heart, eh, Major?" Klaw rasped, slashing his sword.

Nelson blocked the attacking blade, but Klaw's foot suddenly swung out, kicking the injured arm within the sling around the major's neck. Nelson roared with pain and delivered several furious yet skillful saber strokes.

"I'll stick this rifle in his frigging ear if I have to," Becker declared, limping closer.

Lazaro held his Winchester by the barrel and joined his partner.

Nelson's blade clashed with Klaw's again. The one-handed man shoved his sword into Nelson's weapon hard, and stepped in close to his opponent. Klaw's single hand pulled the hook from his belt and quickly shoved the point into the major's side.

Walter Nelson screamed and stumbled away from Klaw, blood pouring from the deep gouge in his ribs. He gasped as the punctured lung robbed him of his breath. Klaw swung the saber attached to his arm overhead. The sharp edge chopped down between the major's shoulder and neck. Cleaving through the collarbone, the blade cut diagonally to Nelson's breastbone, severing his aorta. Klaw put his boot on Major Nelson's corpse and withdrew his sword from the lifeless flesh.

Chapter Seventeen

The people of Cercano Afeitar finally had their treasure hunt. Although Chad Summer was one of the prisoners in the town jail, he didn't offer any information about the gold. The knowledge that the circuit judge would arrive in two weeks, didn't encourage him to be cooperative.

Shovels bit into earth all over Cercano Afeitar. Boards were pried from floors, and the feed store was literally torn apart; every inch of ground was overturned. Yet they failed to find the treasure. Many wondered if the fortune really existed. A small group of impatient men tried to convince Klaw to let them beat the truth out of Summer.

"I'm still the sheriff," the one-handed man told them, as he patted the twin barrels of his Greener. "You folks go back to your digging and leave my prisoners alone."

On the fourth day, they tore the floor boards

from the sheriff's office. At last, they found the chest under four feet of dirt. If the jailhouse had been built two yards to the west, the gold would have been discovered years ago when the stone foundation for the cells was set into the ground.

"Jesus," Becker moaned. "You mean it's been there all the time?"

"That's right, Tom," Klaw commented with an amused grin. "You had a fortune in gold right under your feet."

The treasure was somewhat less than two million dollars in gold bullion, but one million seven hundred thousand didn't prove to be a terrible disappointment. The fortune was divided into shares, the largest belonging to Robert Kehoe and the smallest, ironically, being Klaw's ten thousand.

"There's still plenty left, Klaw," the mayor insisted. "You deserve a larger share after everything you did for us."

"You folks fought to keep your town," Klaw replied. "That's why the bulk of the gold should remain here." He shrugged, "Besides, I don't need any more than I have."

"You know," Kehoe began. "The people in Cercano Afeitar would be happy to see you remain as our sheriff."

"And I'd be happy to do just that," Klaw told him as he unpinned his copper plated badge and handed it to the mayor, "if I didn't have other plans."

"I don't know who we'll get to replace you," Kehoe sighed.

"Why don't you ask Tom Becker if he'd be interested," the one-handed man suggested. "I think he might be."

Klaw led his roan from the livery stable. The saddle bags on his mount were stuffed with gold bars. As he slid his shotgun into its boot, Klaw decided it was lucky for his horse that he'd refused Kehoe's offer. More weight would be a great burden for the animal.

"Klaw," a woman's voice cried. He turned to see Julie hurrying across the street. "Wait, Klaw."

"I wasn't going to leave without saying good-bye," he told her.

"Maybe we can leave together," she suggested. "The stage coach will be arriving in a few hours."

"Where are you going, Julie?"

"Atlanta," she replied. "I want to use my share of the fortune to start a new life—something that doesn't depend on saloons and drunken cowboys. I can't do that here. I'd always be remembered as one of the town whores in Cercano Afeitar."

"I understand," he told her. "I hope everything goes well for you."

"But you won't be going with me to Atlanta?"

Klaw shook his head. "I'm going West to California."

"I see," she whispered, looking down at the ground. "In a way I'm glad you won't be staying here," Julie forced a smile. "At least now I won't have any reason to regret leaving."

She rose on the tips of her toes to press her lips briefly against his. "Good-bye, Klaw."

"Good-bye, Julie."

She turned and hurried to the hotel. Klaw prepared to mount his roan. "Hold on a minute," another familiar voice urged.

Tom Becker limped from the sheriff's office. Klaw smiled as he noticed the star shaped badge on the former outlaw's chest. "Good afternoon,

Sheriff. I see you took the job."

"After you decided to run out on us," Becker growled. "Just where the hell do you think you're going anyway?"

"California," Klaw replied. "I'm going to use my new found wealth to set up a gunsmith shop." He held up the steel hook at the end of his right arm. "I can't do the work myself, but I can afford to set up the business and hire a couple other fellers. I can still supervise the work and, with a little luck, I'll make a nice little profit for myself."

"Profit, hell," Becker snorted. "You just want to have an honest job and make everybody else do the same."

"You'll be a good sheriff, Tom," the one-handed man said sincerely.

"I had a good teacher," Becker shrugged. "By the way, Lazaro bought a buckboard and he went up to the hotel to get Sally. Figured you want to say good-bye to him before they left."

"They plan to go somewhere out of her old man's sphere of influence, huh?"

"Yeah," Becker sighed. "Too bad Sam Clayton is such a hard headed son of a bitch."

As they spoke, Lazaro and Sally rode from the hotel in his buckboard. The hunchback brought the team to a halt and greeted his friends. "We are going now," he said. "Perhaps you will ride with us for awhile, Klaw."

"Sure," the one-handed man agreed. He swung up into the saddle of his mount and turned to Becker. "Take care of yourself, Tom."

"You too, Klaw," the new sheriff replied. "Good luck, Lazaro."

"*Si*," the hunchback nodded. "*Buena suerte.*"

Without warning, a shot interrupted the conversation. Lazaro convulsed violently and toppled from the buckboard. Sally screamed. Becker drew his Tranter, and Klaw pulled his shotgun from its boot. Neil Pierce stepped from the corner of the livery stable, an arrogant smile on his lean rat-like face and a smoking Colt in his hand.

"Drop it, Sheriff," the voice of Clem Smith ordered as he jammed the muzzle of a Winchester roughly into Becker's ribs. "I still remember how you kicked me in the groin with that pegleg of your's, so don't think I won't kill you."

"Same goes for you, Klaw," Joe Felder warned, accenting his threat by cocking the hammer of the revolver that he aimed at the one-handed man. "I owe you a few lumps as well."

Becker let his Tranter fall to the ground. Klaw shoved his Greener back into its boot with a muffled curse. Sally climbed down from the wagon and knelt by Lazaro, as the smugly triumphant Pierce marched forward.

"These boys figure they got a couple scores to settle with you," he announced. "Me, too."

"Old Man Clayton done fired us 'cause of you," Joe snarled, as he moved in front of Klaw, seizing the reins of the roan as he raised his pistol to Klaw's chest.

"I see he's got some good ideas after all," Becker muttered.

"After ten years of working for that old buzzard," Pierce said bitterly, "I lose my job as foreman because of three freaks that decided to play hero."

Klaw leaned back in his saddle. "Killing us won't solve your problem, Pierce," he remarked calmly. "Maybe we can buy our lives."

"Jesus, Klaw," Becker spat. "Don't grovel for

these bastards!''

"He's stalling for time," Clem warned. "Probably hoping the rest of the town will come to their rescue!''

"I've got gold in my saddle bags," Klaw told them.

"Them bags sure are full of something, Neil,'' Joe commented. He pried one open with the frontsight of his revolver. "Hot damn! It's true!''

"How much is there?" Pierce asked, licking his lips eagerly.

"Enough," Klaw replied. "And Tom has a couple thousand dollars in greenbacks.''

"What?" Becker demanded, genuinely confused.

"Don't hold out on these guys," Klaw insisted. "Reach back there and get your wallet for the gents.''

"All right," Becker nodded, slipping his hand under his tunic and sliding it towards his hip pocket.

The .32 caliber S&W suddenly snarled three times. The bullets burned through the gray cloth of Becker's jacket and buried themselves in the chest of the startled Clem Smith. Staggered by the impact of the multiple projectiles, Clem still pulled the trigger of his Winchester, but Becker had already stepped away from the rifle barrel, and the shot hurled into a cloud. Smith dropped his gun, sat down hard and died.

Klaw's hand flashed as he swiftly drew his Remington derringer from his vest pocket. Joe Felder stared up at the over-under muzzles of the diminutive weapon a fragment of a second before it went off in his face. A .41 caliber bullet struck Joe in the right eyesocket and tunneled into his brain. Felder's corpse crumbled, blood oozing from where his eye had once been.

Both Klaw and Becker aimed their guns at Neil Pierce. The former foreman of the Clayton Ranch immediately threw down his Colt and raised his arms in surrender. Klaw glanced down at the prone figure of Lazaro Santos and Sally weeping beside him. A crowd began to gather around them as Klaw pocketed his derringer and dismounted.

"Everybody stay clear of Pierce," he ordered coldly, dragging the shotgun from its scabbard.

"What are you going to do?" Pierce asked nervously.

"Pick up your gun," Klaw demanded as he advanced, sliding his hook into the trigger guard of his Greener.

"No," Pierce cried, kicking his discarded Colt further away. "If you kill me, it'll be cold-blooded murder in front of lots of witnesses!"

"Somebody throw him a gun," the one-handed man said, his eyes resembling two gray pieces of volcanic rock.

"Here," the rough voice of Sam Clayton declared. "And if he doesn't use it, shoot him anyway!"

The rancher hurled an ivory handled revolver to his former employee. Pierce jumped up to grab the gun, his fingers touching the fancy grips. Klaw pulled the trigger of his Greener. The shotgun roared and a burst of 12 gauge buckshot hit Pierce in mid-air. Neil Pierce's body was almost torn in two. His tattered corpse crashed against the side of the livery stable, smearing the wall with blood as it slumped to the ground.

"I was told that Pierce or his men might try something like this today," Clayton stated with a

171

sigh. "I'd hoped to arrive in time to stop him."

"He's stopped now," Klaw remarked grimly. "Not that it'll help Lazaro now."

"Well, maybe the McParlan kid can help him," Tom Becker commented. "He's the closest thing we've got to a doctor."

"You mean he's alive?" Klaw asked hopefully.

"The bullet broke his shoulder," Becker smiled, "but he's gonna be all right."

"What's the matter with you people," Clayton shouted at the crowd. "Didn't you hear the sheriff? Somebody get my future son-in-law to the doctor's office!"

"Looks like the old man's been reconsidering some of his previous notions," Becker mused, as Sam Clayton and his daughter helped Lazaro to his feet.

"Yeah," Klaw smiled. "Maybe I'll stay long enough to attend the wedding."

Epilogue

~~~~~~

David Rolman sat behind his massive mahogany desk, gazing down at the newspaper clippings, file folders and wanted posters spread across his ink-blotter. A prominent tycoon, banker and businessman, Rolman was one of the wealthiest and most powerful men in the country. He was also the head of the American branch of an ambitious and ruthless international organization.

The Euro-American Financial Alliance had been formed two years earlier at a summit meeting in London, England. Their ultimate goal was to control and manipulate the financial and political powers of two continents. Bluntly, they wanted to rule the world. If they could dominate the major monetary systems, monopolize key businesses and trades, and stifle opposition, Rolman felt certain they could succeed.

A small man with a receding hairline, a broad

square face, and soft brown eyes, David Rolman didn't appear to be a shrewd, power-mad conspirator. Yet, he had conceived the Euro-American Financial Alliance shortly after the War Between the States. Rolman believed if an organization had been able to make *both* the Union and Confederacy dependent on it for financial survival, that organization would have had the United States of America in its pocket by the conclusion of the war, regardless of which side emerged the victor.

There would be more wars in the future—both civil conflicts and wars among nations. Next time, Rolman vowed, his organization would be ready to seize control. He'd searched throughout five countries for the right men to comprise the Euro-American Financial Alliance. Now, all they had to do was get their organizational branches ready and wait.

However, Rolman's plans for setting up a base of operations in Great Ford, Colorado had failed. He sent the Claxton Detective Agency to investigate the cause. Seven months later, the detectives reported back to Rolman. They had discovered that one man had been responsible for the Euro-American Financial Alliance's failure.

How had a single individual—and, according to the reports, a man with only one hand—utterly destroyed their organization in Colorado? How much did he know about the Alliance? Would he stand in the way of their plans in the future?

A knock on the office door drew his attention from the paperwork before him. "Come in," he said.

Two remarkably different figures entered. A short, wiry man dressed in a pin-striped suit removed his derby and bowed politely. "Mister

174

Rolman, I presume." His voice was flavored by a British accent.

"You must be Mister Wislow," Rolman replied.

The Englishman nodded.

His companion remained silent. A startling figure, the man was nearly six feet nine inches tall. The face framed by shoulder length black hair could have been carved from seasoned red oak. A hawkish nose jutted between cold blue eyes, and his stern hard mouth seemed incapable of a smile. Although he wore a suit-jacket, the giant's feet were encased in deerskin boots. Rolman noticed the wide, steel blade of a tomahawk thrust in the man's belt.

"You, of course, are Mister Tracker," Rolman said.

"Just Tracker," the towering figure replied in a deep, wooden voice. "It is not who I am, but what I am."

"I know," the tycoon declared, leaning back in his chair. "That's why you're here. You two are said to be the greatest man-hunters in the world."

"Well, I've never worked with Tracker before," Wislow replied, "but I'm certain he must be good."

"He is," Rolman assured the Briton. "And he's hunted men in the American West. That's why I hired both of you to handle this job."

"And what exactly is our job, sir?"

"I want you to find this man," Rolman answered, handing Wislow a wanted poster bearing Klaw's name and description. "I don't care how long it takes, or how much it costs. I want you to find him and kill him."

"Not to worry, Mr. Rolman," Wislow assured

him, glancing at the poster. "This . . . Klaw . . . is as good as dead."

Tracker nodded in agreement.